Acknowledgements

Where do I start? When I started writing this novel, I was going through a tough time. I was in college, working all hours of the night in a news station and then waking up early the next morning for school. On top of all of that, I was heartbroken. Before I developed Ashley, Mason and friends, I wrote an *entire* non-fiction book about getting over heartbreak. It just didn't fit. I wanted something that could be related to, thus, *Bride Not to Be* was born! It took long nights and early mornings to finish this, and I'm very happy to say it's finally finished! I would like to thank the people that helped me along my journey, those who read and edited my book in its beginning stages, those who told me what was great and what didn't really sound good. Ya'll know I put some crazy stuff in this book at the beginning! Thank you all for your honesty. I would like to thank the readers who supported me from the start, from keeping up with my blog to telling me how excited you were for the book's release. I would also like to thank those who helped dry my eyes as I figured my life out! My mother, thank you for always supporting me and helping me get over some of my roughest times. To the owner of the dress shop, you were the first person I believed when you told me that I would be okay. Thank You. To Dawn, Annie, Antoine, my best friends Brandi and Fatima, and my sisters Angelica and Mia, thank you guys for listening to me whine throughout this process- sometimes for hours and still being there! And finally, I would like to thank myself for not putting a hole in the wall through finishing this darn thing! Nobody ever told me it would be this hard! But I'm happy and proud of what my life journey has allowed me to accomplish. I love you all!

To my first love, thank you for helping me become the woman that I am today.

Bride Not to Be

Copyright © 2015 D. D. Richard

www.bridenottobebook.com

I wanted sex. Plain and simple.

But it sure as hell couldn't be with the guy who stood in front of me.

I looked at the hunk I was dumb enough to go home with for the night. After three martinis and two vodka shots, I had lost all of my good judgment. It's funny how a few drinks could cloud reality. I sat up on the hunk's bed, wondering what I had just gotten myself into. It was now morning, we were so tired by the time we got to his house the night before that we both fell asleep. I glanced at the clock and panicked when I saw that it was 8:01. The hunk wanted to get laid but I wanted to get out of there-fast.

I rolled my eyes in disgust before speaking to my sort of one night stand. "If I'm not mistaken, didn't you just say this was your mother's house?" I said as he stood in the mirror admiring himself. Standing 6'1, glistening skin and a great package, I was disappointed that my standards had stooped low enough to go home with someone I didn't know. I was so drunk that I also didn't notice his mother's minivan as I stumbled in front of the house. I should have known something wasn't right, because he drove *my* car to his house. The guy laughed and then began to look nervous. "No, this is not my mom's house. She lives upstairs, the basement is all mine." He said with a naughty grin.

Yeah right.

I cursed myself as I scrambled to put my clothes on. Now that I had sobered up, there was no way I was giving it up to this guy. I turned to look at the hunk, realizing what a mistake he was. "Let me guess, this is your house, you just gave her the entire upstairs right?" I said.

"Yeah, that's right. How did you know?" he laughed. He had every right to laugh, he was smart enough to bring a girl home, and I was dumb enough to become swayed by his good looks that I didn't pay attention to the fact that he still lived with his mom.

Jokes on me I guess.

"Well, thanks for the good time, but I have to get to work." I said as I ran to the door. I stopped myself before exiting. "What was your name again?"

The guy laughed before answering. "What do you want my name to be?"

I shook my head. Right.

"Yeah, thanks. Bye!" I said as I walked out of the door to his basement apartment. I immediately stopped in my tracks once I noticed a middle aged woman carrying several grocery bags in her hand. Her matronly looks signaled that she was the hunk's mother, who just so happened to catch me during my walk of shame. We exchanged awkward glances as his mother tilted her head to the side, wondering who the hell I was. I smiled, spotted my car and rushed towards it, heading home in order to get ready for work. I looked down at my watch and sighed as I realized that I only had one hour, and I also had a very important meeting. Great. I was embarrassed, hung-over, and I also had to make big decisions today. As I drove off, I laughed at myself and swore not to go home with another stranger.

****

"Ashley!"

I stopped replaying this morning's events in my head and realized that I was in the middle of a meeting. It was my turn to present my proposal. My best friend Randy was staring at me, analyzing me with a face that looked like he had just seen a ghost.

Randy leaned over and whispered. "It's your turn to present Ashley." Oh, and wipe that smirk off of your face, you know you are starting with the cure Diabetes campaign."

"Uh-Huh, Gotcha". I said.

At the tender age of 28, I was an executive in a prominent advertising firm. I was beautiful, successful-and lonely. Between my various one-night stands and numerous horrible dates, I hadn't had a successful relationship in years. The good news was, in addition to my successful advertising career, I had one of the top wedding consulting firms in the state of California-Bella Bridal Consulting. When it came to my own life however, love didn't exist in my vocabulary. Although I had two great careers, I was looking forward to being a single cat lady for the rest of my life. My biological clock was ticking fast.

"That presentation was a-m-a-z-i-n-g!" My best friend Randy came running over to my office after the meeting was over. I jokingly dusted my shoulder off. "Thanks!" I paused, realizing that Randy had come over to my desk for a reason. He had a blind date planned for me that night, but I didn't feel like going.

"So?" He looked at me with his big brown eyes. I ignored his advances. I didn't want to go.

"Yeah, So." I replied hastily.

Randy raised an eyebrow and slammed his folder on my desk. "You know what I'm talking about! Tonight at the Plaza. You've got a date with my cousin."

I frowned. "I know what you are talking about. I'm not going. Plus, he's like your fifth cousin. That doesn't even count. If you would have known what I went through this morning, you would understand why I'm saying no."

"Yes, you are going." Randy said, ignoring my comment. I shook my head and looked down at the work on my desk.

Randy could tell I wasn't paying him any attention. He suddenly raised his voice in order to get through to me. "I said, you are going!"

The entire office looked over into the doorway of my office. Everybody already knew I was capable of being a complete bitch, so it didn't really surprise anyone when I blurted "What the hell are y'all looking at? The damn meeting was over ten minutes ago, so stop watching me!" The employees in the office quickly shuffled and returned to their duties.

I looked at Randy, who was confused as to why I would cancel a date I had seemed so excited about earlier in the week. "Look Ran, I'm just not up to it."

Randy laughed. "Girl, it's time to get out. I know you are tired of Mr. Purp. Batteries can't do what the real *thang* can do." Randy said as he began to roll his groin in circles. I laughed at the way Randy poked fun of my purple vibrator. He always knew how to make me smile. I softly punched him on his shoulder. If only he knew about my failed attempt to hook up with someone earlier that day.

I looked at Randy, still not convinced that I should go out once again. "Well, I'll have you to know that Mr. Purp and I are doing just fine." I said.

Randy picked up his folder and headed towards the door. "Well, Ash, it's time to get over that! You are a gorgeous woman. You don't even have kids! Time is ticking."

I rolled my eyes. "Whatever".

"So, tonight at 8?" Randy wasn't giving up. His persistence was one of the things I loved about him being my best friend.

I smiled coyly. "Sure, tonight at 8."

By the time evening rolled around, I wasn't ready to go out, but I promised Randy that I would give his cousin a chance. The fact that I would even go out with my best friend's cousin showed just how desperate I had become.

As I got dressed for the blind date, I admired myself in the mirror. "Damn girl." I said aloud. I had to admit, I was looking fine. I smiled as I fingered the body hugging black dress that graced my petite 5'4 frame. I shook my dark brown shoulder length hair as I applied the hottest red lipstick I could find. If I was going to go out, I had to do it right. I secretly hoped that if he took me home, there wouldn't be a minivan in the driveway.

I turned around and slapped my butt playfully. "You look good girl!" I said to myself. Randy would be proud. I headed towards the door, hoping that I would be able to put Mr. Purp away for the night.

****

The *Plaza* Restaurant was one of the hottest eateries in LA. People across the country came just to sit at the restaurants gold laced tables. Celebrities, Politicians and the very wealthy frequented the establishment, sometimes dropping over $600 just for a meal.

"Glad my cheap ass isn't paying," I said to myself as I looked at the menu and waited for my 'blind date' to arrive. He was late and I was hungry. The smooth jazz and hushed voices around the restaurant gave a very romantic ambiance.

I glanced up from my menu and noticed that a good looking server approached me with a pen and paper in hand, ready to take my order. He looked fancy.

"Good evening, wine?" The server asked.

I pointed at the most expensive option on the menu. This guy was going to pay for not showing up on time. Hell, he brought me here, I'm sure he could afford it.

The server wrote my selection on the small piece of paper. "Are you waiting for someone?"

"Not for long!" I snapped back. My bitch side always seemed to surface at the wrong times.

Before the server could walk away, a tall handsome man walked up behind him. "One moment please, I would like to have a bottle of what she just ordered," he crooned. His voice sounded like music. His smooth skin graced the three piece suit on his muscular-yet slim body. I was in awe.

"Brandon." He said as he held his hand out and smiled, showing all 32 of his perfect white teeth.

"Ashley." I scoffed. He was sexy as hell, but he was still late. I didn't say anything though, for the sake of Randy.

"How could Randy keep you away for so long? He never told me he had such a beautiful friend. I'm starting to think he wanted you for himself."

I squinted my eyes. I wasn't impressed.

"Yeah, thanks."

By the look on my face, Brandon could sense that I was a little upset over his tardiness.

"I'm sorry for being a little late. I had a meeting and I remembered that Randy had the "no contact rule" before meeting you. Give me a chance, will ya?"

I knew why Randy did that. I was a tough cookie sometimes, he didn't want me to scare the poor guy away before meeting him.

I smiled. "Understood." Brandon was really cute, but I couldn't help but wonder if he lived in his mother's basement.

Brandon started showing all of those perfect teeth once again. "May I add how gorgeous you look tonight? Or should I say, sexy."

I never thought of myself as completely sexy. Maybe a librarian kind of sexy, but not "drop your boxers" type sexy. This was becoming awkward.

"Thank you, you look pretty great yourself."

"I know." Brandon said.

Oh gosh.

I was really growing restless at this point. Brandon was right, Randy should have kept me a little secret. This date needed to end immediately. I didn't need to waste my time on another horrific date.

"You know? Not 'Thank you'?"

Brandon burst out laughing. "I knew that would get you going! Thank you, Ashley. Now how about we enjoy dinner?

I smiled, a sense of humor was just what I needed.

"Alright, let's eat." I said to him as I picked up my fork. I began to hope that his sense of humor remained after he found out the price of the wine I ordered.

Once dinner was over, I was completely full. It was good but it wasn't worth all the money Brandon probably ended up spending. I've had better at mom and pop shops down South. However, after I got over my rut, Brandon and I actually started to have a good time.

As the end of the evening approached, I rushed through my brain to try and find the right words to say as we sat outside of the restaurant. I hadn't dated successfully in years and my date dictionary had completely expired. The only words I really knew how to say after a date were

"Take me home". I know, what a shame. Brandon looked at me absent minded as if he were waiting for me to say something first. Confused on what to say, I blurted out the first words that came to mind.

"Uh…I had a nice time?"

Brandon continued to stare with a blank drawn on his face. Oh shit. I searched through my word bank to find something else to say. What came out was even more elementary than the first.

"Uhhh…we should do this again sometime."

Brandon continued to stare at me. Damn, every word I said made me look stupid. I opened my mouth again to say something else. Before I could, he grabbed the back of my head and shoved his tongue down my throat. I pulled away, surprised that this guy was so clumsy. It was not sexy at all and I was completely turned off at that point.

"What the hell?" I said while gasping for air.

"Sorry. Randy said you hadn't gotten any in a while."

"Randy said *what*?!"

Brandon looked at me smiling, this time cautiously. Randy knew damn well that sex was the least of my problems-well, sorta. I snickered as I realized my best friend basically pimped me out to his cousin. This was worse than the night before. Brandon paused.

"Listen, he said that you were drier than the Sahara, and that you needed a real man to help you put down Mr. Blurp-or something like that. I thought this was what you wanted." Brandon said.

I was furious, not only that Randy had practically told his cousin that I had no sex life, but also that this guy had completely butchered the name of my favorite vibrator.

I pushed Brandon away. "Okay, this date is over, thanks for the CPR though."

Brandon looked disappointed. "I'm so sorry, I really did have a nice time. Would you like to try again?"

"No. Thank. You." I said as I quickly walked towards the first cab I saw and abruptly closed the door. I felt the need to say one more thing so I opened the door and yelled behind Brandon as he got into his car.

"And it's Mr. Purp!"

I slammed the door as the taxi quickly drove away. I was going to kill Randy the next day.

****

"You are such a beautiful bride!" I looked at Melissa, one of my clients who was trying on her wedding dress. I loved my job as a wedding consultant-probably even better than working in advertising, which is why skipped work to honor Melissa's last minute request to accompany her to a bridal dress shop. The romance surrounding weddings helped me believe in love-slightly. After last night's events, I was determined that I would never find love.

Melissa giggled. "You like it?"

"I love it! I think we can all agree that it's gorgeous." I turned around to look for the approval of Melissa's bridesmaids. They all nodded their head in agreement.

One thing I loved about planning weddings was that I was able to see someone happy. A wedding is such a special day, and any woman would be blessed to experience it. Because I had never gotten married, I somewhat lived vicariously through the lives of other brides. Luckily, I never told them that, or I would just look like the crazy lady who crashes the weddings of others because she couldn't have her own.

The room suddenly got quiet. We were already in the bridal shop for three hours, waiting for Melissa to find her dream wedding dress. At this point, everyone had secretly begun to get restless.

"This is it!" Melissa cried out happily. "I say YES!"

I breathed a sigh of relief as the coos filled the room and the women embraced the bride to be in her dress of choice. This was one of the best parts of the job. I turned to the bridal shop owner and barked out directions.

"Make sure we can get alterations within the next few weeks, there isn't much time left before the wedding. Make it happen."

The shop owner smirked at me and shuffled to the front of the shop.

After a few minutes, Melissa was now in her regular clothes, beaming.

"It keeps getting better and better! My wedding is going to be perfect because of you Ash."

I blew her a smooch as she stepped closer to hug me. She was a happy client and a happy client meant I was happy.

Outside of the shop, I called out to Melissa who was practically galloping to her car in happiness. After all this time we had spent together, I had yet to meet her fiancé and I started to get curious. "When am I going to meet the lucky guy?" I asked.

"Soon!" Melissa said. "Why don't we plan the catering tasting according to his arrival in town? He's never home-big shot business guy."

I didn't care to hear how successful this guy was. Although I liked Melissa, A part of me just wanted to make sure he even existed. She never talked about him, even when I asked. I looked over my shoulder and saw that Randy was right on time for lunch.

I began to speak hastily so that I could meet Randy. "Uh, sure! Sounds great, see you soon!"

I exchanged goodbyes with Melissa and headed towards Randy's car. I had every curse word in the book ready for Randy on a silver platter. He set me up with his cousin, his cousin practically humped me on the sidewalk, and I was pissed. Did men even know how to be romantic anymore?

Randy smiled and waved as I sat inside of his car. I convinced him to skip work as well so that I could have all the time I needed to curse him out.

"Randolph, what the fu-"

Randy stopped me before I could finish. "What did you do to him?" he said. Randy seemed excited, which confused me because the date was a complete bust.

"Huh?"

"He said you both had a great time."

"Excuse me?"

I didn't know where he was going. If I recall, the date ended horribly, and I sure as hell didn't remember Brandon pleasing me at all that night. It was me and Mr. Purp. Unlike my past few dates, that little vibrator was reliable.

Randy put the car in reverse and turned on a loud hip-hop track in true Randy fashion.

"He wants another date." Randy said.

I was confused. "Did he say anything else?"

Randy thought for a moment. "No. Why?"

I figured that Randy knew exactly what happened, but was feeling guilty for basically pimping me out. I decided to let it go-for now. Randy's phone buzzed. I didn't pay attention to the interference until Randy shoved the phone in my face. It was from Donald, our boss at the advertising firm.

"Come to office, now. Bring Ashley. I know you two are together."

Randy shrugged the text off and pressed on the gas so that we could head to the office and see what was up. "Well, what do you say, tomorrow night? He's a busy man." Once again, Randy was rushing me to answer him about a date.

I figured why the hell not. I didn't have anything better to do, and it was safe to say that I didn't think Brandon lived with his mom.

"Well, okay!" I said. I thought to myself that Brandon had better not drown me with his tongue this time, but he could definitely get it from me.

We entered the office to the advertising firm, and for the first time in the nine years I had worked at Briggs Solutions Incorporated, it was amazingly quiet. No shuffling employees, no busy meetings being held, nothing. Everybody was just sitting quietly at their desks. It seemed weird to me, especially for a weekday. I could spot Donald from his office and headed towards his way. *He caught us playing hooky,* I thought to myself. I didn't know how Randy skipped out on work, but I called in sick since I didn't have any vacation days left. Randy was by my side and was nervous as well. I glanced over to my best friend.

"Oh shit, this can't be good." I said.

Randy answered me while still nervously looking straight ahead.

"Don't rub it in, just be cool." He said.

As we entered the office, I was suddenly pushed by one of the secretaries-she was crying. At that point, I was trying to figure out what the hell was going on.

Donald stared at Randy and I as we entered the room.

"Ashley."

"Yes, Don?"

Donald looked over to Randy. "Randolph."

Randy looked scared. "Donald."

Donald sat up straight in his chair and cleared his throat.

"I know the two of you weren't at work today, which is fine. But have you two been watching the news?"

Randy and I looked at each other. We were definitely relieved that we weren't being fired for partaking in midday lunches and wedding planning instead of going to work.

I fessed up. "No, we haven't."

Tears filled Donald's eyes. "Mr. Briggs is dead. Massive heart attack."

Randy and I were overblown with surprise. The owner of one of the largest advertising firms in the country had just died, and he didn't have a family heir to take over-which meant, Briggs Solutions could soon be no more. Nobody ever knew Mr. Briggs, the only thing the company really knew about him was the ongoing rumor that he was too busy fooling around with women more than half his age to ever think about starting a family.

I looked down to the ground. "That's very unfortunate." I said.

Randy was quiet.

Donald looked towards the sky and smiled. "Yes, very unfortunate…well, reports say he died with three women in his bed, so I'm sure he didn't suffer."

Although the situation was sad, it was hard not to hold back a chuckle. It was known that Mr. Briggs had a plethora of women, even at age 65. I quickly snapped back into serious mode.

Randy cut to the chase.

"I'm sorry for the loss. But are we losing our jobs? Is that why you brought us in here?"

I scoffed at Randy for being so inconsiderate at a time like this. The people in the office were quiet because they all knew we were about to be unemployed. I was disappointed in Randy for his lack of compassion.

Donald squinted his eyes at Randy, looked over at me, and answered. "Yes, you could lose your jobs-unless…"

"Unless *what?*" I thought to myself. I didn't enjoy death, but I liked my job. If anything, I could plan weddings full time, but I enjoyed the cut throat nature of the advertising business. Donald needed to speak up-and fast.

Once again, Donald cleared his throat-a little harder this time. His habits irritated the hell out of me. "You two are some of the most successful executives here at Briggs Solutions Incorporated."

Randy and I looked at each other in delight. We knew we were pretty damn good at what we do.

Randy grew irritated.

"Look, if this is the way you are going to lay us off.." Randy started.

I stopped Randy in his tracks. He needed to shut up.

I looked back at Donald. "So, what does that mean for us?"

"Well, without Mr. Briggs, there can't be a Briggs Solutions Incorporated, unless someone else steps up to the plate."

I gasped with relief. Maybe we weren't going to lose our jobs after all. I grew excited, because I could feel a promotion coming.

"I'm confused Don. What are you trying to say?" Randy called out. I was a little confused too, but I was patient enough to see what our boss was going to say, unlike Randy.

Don rubbed his nose hard and I watched a small booger land on the sheets of paper sprawled across his desk. Gross.

Don smiled. "That's me, *I'm* stepping up to the plate. It's about time, I've paid my dues."

Well whoopdie damn-doo Don! Is what I really wanted to say, but I instead smiled and replied in a hushed tone. "Congratulations Don." I was also beginning to get a little irritated-I couldn't believe he brought me and Randy in his office to tell us that not only did the owner of the firm die, we could be losing our jobs-unless he decided that he wanted to take over the company.

"Let me finish." Donald said. Randy and I both got quiet.

"Once I step up to the plate as CEO, one of you must take my place."

Randy and I looked at each other.

Don laughed. "My job you assholes. One of you, my job. Get what I'm saying here?"

Randy side-eyed Don. "Well, *asshole*, if the company is going to be okay, why don't you go out there and say something? It's mayhem out there, way too quiet!"

I laughed quietly at Randy's reference to the busy demeanor of an advertising firm. It was funny how silence in an advertising firm meant that something was wrong.

"I just wanted to see how everyone would react." Don announced as he shrugged his shoulders.

It was official, Don *was* the complete *asshole*.

I elbowed Randy.

"So, what does that mean for us?" I said again.

"It means, one of you will soon have my job. It's up to you how you take that."

I co uld feel my power meter going up tenfold. Once Don becomes CEO, *I* could be the managing partner of Briggs Solutions Incorporated.

But so could Randy.

Shit.

Randy glanced my way and cocked his head to one side in curiosity. I wasn't paying attention to his thoughts. I was too busy thinking about how I could redecorate Don's bland office to realize that I could possibly be competing against my best friend.

I then made a mental note to avoid skipping work to meet a bride-or *at least* watch the news while I'm out, just to be on the safe side.

****

I couldn't get Randy out of my head the next day as I entered the park for a picnic date with Brandon. I hadn't spoken to Randy yet, but I was sure he would call by the end of the day to see how date #2 went with his cousin. Brandon and I had decided that the late night dinner date may not have been the best thing to do after the other evening. He said he wanted to redeem himself and be polite.

Damn. I was trying to get some, but I guess it could wait.

I spotted Brandon sitting on a bright yellow blanket next to a tree that was small enough for us to see the sun, but large enough to provide the right amount of shade. He looked amazing, just like the other night.

As I walked closer to Brandon, my mind began to trail into a memory I once shared at this same park, a decade ago.

"On our next date, I'm going to take you on a horse and carriage around the park." I looked into Mason's eyes and saw the sparkle that I had not seen in anyone before.

"I don't like a horse and carriage," I said. "It's cruel to have a horse carry people like that, but my mother always told me that what horses were made for."

Mason laughed.

"Well, I guess I won't take you on a horse and carriage."

I smiled, looked into his eyes and knew that I had found the one.

I stopped myself in my tracks as I had a flashback to a time from long ago. This was the exact area my ex Mason and I used to hang out during college. He was my first love, in fact, he was my first everything, including my first heartbreak. He dumped me once he graduated from college-walking out on a wedding that we were planning together. I was crushed for years, I actually haven't completely gotten over it. However, I moved on and began to take on my life as a serial dater. It was the past, and it was time I let it go. I did sometimes wish that he had gotten hit by a bus. Getting hit by a bus was how I described my pain, and I wanted him to feel it too. I shook the flashback off and approached Brandon waving my face, pretending to be really hot. We had to move to another area-quickly.

"Geeze, it's hot over here! Can we move?" I looked at Brandon, who was wearing a light blue linen shirt, perfect for the sunny day.

Brandon smiled. "I was looking for a place that had shade, but if you insist, we shall move elsewhere my lady."

His lady. I liked that.

We moved to a spot that wouldn't make me think about the past. Sure, it was the same park, but it didn't take much for me to focus. I opened the picnic basket and retrieved a sandwich.

"I like you." Brandon said.

I glanced up and could see Brandon looking at me with compassion as his hand graced my shoulder.

"Yeah, you showed me the other day." I laughed.

Brandon flashed his beautiful teeth. Damn, I loved those teeth.

"This picnic is wonderful," I said. Being with Brandon helped me forget about the previous day at work. Don dropped a bomb on Randy and I both, and I'm sure neither of us knew how to handle it.

Brandon brushed a piece of hair out of my face, and looked me straight in the eye. "And so are you."

"Let's pretend the other day didn't happen. Let's start over. Deal?"

"Deal."

I completely forgot about just a random hookup with Brandon. I thought to myself I may actually like this guy, however, although he requested, it would be really hard to forget about his chokehold kiss.

****

The next morning, I was lying in my bed, staring at the ceiling. The sun rays shined into my bedroom-which fit my contentment. Thanks to Randy's consistent attitude, I was beginning to actually *like* someone, and he liked me too! It was now Sunday, and I still hadn't heard from Randy. Was he upset? Was he thinking about what he would do? Should I call him first? My phone rang and I jumped over to my nightstand, thinking that it was my best friend calling to talk about the other day. I looked at the ID screen and sighed when I saw Melissa's name.

Melissa's bubbly voice shouted through the line.

"Hey!"

I was disappointed that it wasn't Randy, but it was nice to talk to Melissa.

"Hey, Melissa" I said.

Melissa didn't give me any time to say anything else before she started her bridal rant.

"I need someone to help me pick out my stationary! I can't decide whether it the laser cut or the imprinted invitations work best. Help?"

I looked at the clock, it was 7am. It was way too early. I made a note to myself to change the contact clause in my contract for future brides. I couldn't help myself though, I loved what I did. I got up and began to get dressed to meet Melissa.

"I'm on the way."

"Great! See you soon!" Melissa immediately hung up.

As usual, I admired Melissa's beauty as I approached *Sammies Patio Cafe* on Sunset Boulevard. Melissa's hair was pulled back in an elegant bun, and she wore a white sundress. She actually looked like she was about to have a beach wedding.

I didn't even completely sit in my chair before Melissa began talking.

"So, I have this invitation that I don't think my mom will really approve of, and she's paying, so I need to-"

Melissa paused and looked at me with a worried look on her face.

"Ash?" What's wrong?

"Oh, who, me?" I looked around the café thinking she was speaking to someone else, even though she said my name and was looking directly at me. I didn't think my face showed that I had something on my mind. Regardless, I was the planner, she was the client. She didn't need to fix me.

"I'm fine Melissa," I said.

Melissa smacked her lips and took a sip of her mimosa.

"You don't look fine, my invitations can wait. Talk!"

For some reason, I felt more comfortable with Melissa than my other brides. The weight of what happened at work burdened me. I couldn't talk to Brandon about it, Randy was his cousin. Melissa could probably give me the non-biased opinion that I needed.

I looked down at my plate of blueberry pancakes. "Just work."

Melissa gasped. "Not Bella Bride, right?"

I smiled slightly. "No, not Bella Bride."

I told Melissa the entire story of what happened with me and Randy in Don's office. By the end of the story, she seemed depleted.

"What are you going to do?" She gasped.

I didn't know. A part of me wanted to throw the whole thing and give it to Randy just for the sake of our friendship. He would do the same for me, I think.

"Nothing, for now." I said. It felt good to talk to someone about my dilemma. Melissa started become more than just a client to me, I enjoyed her company.

Melissa smiled, her elegant face beaming. "It will work out." She said. "Whenever you are unsure of something, follow your heart."

Melissa paused and took a look at my blueberry pancakes. "May I?" she said as she stuck her fork out towards my plate with an expression that said "you better say yes." I couldn't deny her with the fork practically already on my plate so I obliged. Melissa put the pancake in her mouth and began to speak.

"Bubba's coming into town! It's time to meet him."

I froze. "Bubba? Is that your dog?"

Melissa laughed. No silly! My fiancé!

Finally.

I high fived her and laughed to myself. She had a real fiancé after all.

"Let's meet Bubba!" I said.

Melissa picked up her phone and smiled.

"He's outside! I'm so excited, I haven't seen him in weeks!"

Melissa grabbed my hand and pulled me toward the curb away from the restaurant. By the time we had reached the street, I realized that we hadn't paid for our brunch.

"Um, Melissa, we didn't pay." I said.

Melissa was so happy to see 'Bubba' that she didn't even acknowledge me. I politely pulled away, and headed back towards the restaurant.

"What are you doing?" Melissa said.

I laughed. "Well unless you want to go to jail for walking out on the food, I suggest I go back and pay for brunch. It's on me."

Melissa beamed, happy for the free food and the chance to see her man.

"Great! Hurry!" Melissa said.

I rushed inside and couldn't find the server anywhere. I ended up flagging the bus boy down to fetch the server. My phone vibrated and I saw the text from Melissa:

"G2G! You can meet him at catering tasting 2morow!"

I texted her back and said that was fine, and reminded her that I would be slightly late. Since last week's saga at the office, I felt it was best to be there as much as possible.

****

While at work the next day, I couldn't concentrate on the work piled on my desk. All I could do was look for Randy, who was usually on time for work but hadn't appeared. I couldn't wait any longer, so I took it upon myself to wait at his desk. Randy soon arrived, looking disheveled. Once he spotted me sitting at his desk, he smiled.

"Hey Ran!" I said.

Randy studied me. "Hey Ash."

I began speaking before he could say anything else.

"Look. About the other day. I-"

Randy stopped me mid-sentence. "That was crazy huh? It's enough that Mr. Briggs dropped dead in a bed full of women. Not only that, but I'm up against my best friend for one of the top positions in the company."

My thoughts were quickly coming to me, I couldn't risk losing Randy. We had been friends since college. In fact, I was the one who told him about coming to work for Briggs Solutions Incorporated when I first got the job. We were in this together.

"Ran, you deserve this, you put in a lot of hard work." I said with a half smile on my face.

"So did you Ash. You would make a great managing partner." Randy said. He seemed to be warming up a little. I had to admit, it was quite awkward. I decided that no promotion was better than a friendship.

"Forget this Ran. Let's go out tonight and drink. I can snag you some girls, but I don't think I will be in need of your wingman services this time around." I had a big smile on my face, thinking about the fun Brandon and I had on our picnic.

Randy suddenly forgot about the problems we had at work and immediately switched gears- back into the Randy before the promotion fiasco.

"I knew it! I knew you would like him."

I smiled. "I do."

Randy gyrated his hips in a way that made me question his sexuality.

"Time to put Mr. Purp away!"

I rolled my eyes, chuckling. "Not quite yet." I had to hold out for this one.

Randy laughed. "Hopefully sooner than later."

A slight grin ran across my face. I still hadn't cursed Randy out for what happened on me and Brandon's first date. With everything going on, it really didn't matter anymore. Everything was slowly getting back to normal between Randy and I. My phone vibrated with a text from Melissa. She was reminding me about the catering tasting.

"Don't forget, tasting today!"

I wondered if she knew that I didn't need her updates, I had my own smartphone. My annoyance didn't show in the text I sent back to her:

"Gotcha, on my way right after work!"

I looked over at Randy, who was now motioning me to get out of his seat.

"Go work. Remember, this firm could crumble at any moment. Don't want Don to see you sitting your lazy ass in my chair."

I laughed and playfully hit Randy on his shoulder.

"Shutup. Are we okay?"

Randy looked me and smiled.

"We are okay." He said.

"Good." I rushed back to my office before Don could see me. I was anxious for the work day to end so that I could meet Melissa for the tasting.

****

I walked into *Entrée Soiree* catering with a smile on my face. I never turned down free food, and the fact that I was with my favorite bride helped a lot. "This is tasty!" I heard Melissa as I walked in. She was delighted with the peanut butter chicken skewers, but she then quickly frowned. "Bubba is allergic to peanuts". She said. The catering manager assured Melissa that they would be able to find something to her liking.

"What about calamari?" The manager said. Melissa stared at the ceiling before shaking her head. "Octopus, yuck. Bubba will be here in a second, maybe he can decide." The catering manager ran to the kitchen to retrieve the other menu items. Because I overheard the entire conversation entering the building, I walked up to Melissa and said jokingly, "You know it's your day right? Who cares what the groom wants." As usual, Melissa was delighted to see me.

"Ash!"

I smiled at Melissa and sat in the chair next to her. I accompanied Melissa with her maid of honor Andrea and Melissa's mother. Andrea and I exchanged glances. Andrea was Melissa's best friend since age five, and she seemed to be jealous of the relationship Melissa and I began to create. I smiled at her and quickly looked the other way. I had to admit, I was anxious to meet 'Bubba'. I pictured who a 'Bubba' would look like, and secretly hoped that Melissa's fiancé didn't look like the illustration I drew in my head. As I wondered what Melissa's fiancé looked like, the catering manager appeared from the back with a tray of cocktail shrimp in her hand. Melissa's phone vibrated, and she smiled.

"Ash, can you please go tell the catering manager I don't like shrimp? I could have sworn I marked shrimp as a 'no' on the form. I'm going to get Bubba!"

"Gotcha." I replied as I turned around to stop the caterer in her tracks.

A few minutes later, I could hear Melissa shrieking as if she were a kid getting ice cream. Whoever this Bubba guy was, he sure did make her happy. "She doesn't like shrimp." I told the catering manager. "Could you please find another item?"

"Sure." The manager said. She angrily rushed to the back once more. As she trailed off, I snatched a piece of cocktail shrimp and shoved it in my mouth.

"Ashley! Here he is!"

My mouth was still full and my back was turned, so I was caught a little off guard when Melissa called my name. I quickly spun on my heels to meet Ashley's infamous Bubba.

When I saw who stood in front of me, I had to blink twice to believe what I was seeing.

It was him.

"Ashley, meet Mason. Mason, meet Ashley."

Silence filled the room.

Melissa chucked. "It's Bubba, Ashley!"

I knew who the hell he was. He was Mason, the Mason that broke my heart ten years ago. I tried my best to conjure up the strength to say something, but I couldn't. In fact, it felt like my heart was breaking all over again.

Even after all this time.

Mason looked at me, eyes wide with surprise. I couldn't believe we had all gone this far without identifying the fiancé to the wedding planner. I was shaken.

The catering manager ran out of the kitchen, this time with vegetables in her hand.

"I have cucumber quiche! How about that?"

I wasn't paying attention to her, because I couldn't think.

Melissa must have not noticed the tension, for she smiled and ran back to the catering manager to taste the selection.

"Hello Ashley." Mason said, extending his hand out to me, as if we had just met.

I looked Mason up and down. He still looked great. His white button up shirt and gray slacks gave away that he must have just gotten off of work. His hair was cut perfectly. His skin still had that glow and it shined as the sun beamed through the window. I began to wonder if his breath still smelled like a baby's in the morning, I began to wonder if he still wore the same Old Spice at night. My mind was completely gone.

I extended my hand out to his and played along.

"Pleasure to meet you, Mason."

By then, Melissa had ran up to us and was delighted that her fiancé and wedding planner had finally become acquainted.

"There she is Bubba! This is the girl I have been talking to you about for so long!"

Mason simply looked my way and smiled. He still had it.

"I'm sure she is doing a great job." Mason said as he looked at Melissa with love in his eyes.

I couldn't believe this was happening to me. L.A. is supposed to be big. What the hell was he still doing in L.A.? People don't just run into each other, unless they are in Hollywood. I was a damn advertising agent, I couldn't believe I was even still in the catering shop.

"Give her a kiss Mason!" Our entire families were standing in Sycamore park, the same day of Mason's graduation. I turned my head after Mason's mother shouted the request as we took pictures. "Give Mason a kiss Ashley!" his mom shouted one more. I obliged, and gave him a simple kiss on the cheek while my eyes were

closed. As I opened my eyes, there Mason was on bended knee. He held a silver ring box in his hand that held a beautiful princess cut engagement ring. Caught by surprise, I started screaming. My screaming session must have lasted long, because Mason soon cut me off and said "Well, what do you say?" "Yes!" I shouted. Mason put the ring on my finger and I gave him a kiss, this time on the lips. We were going to be Mr. and Mrs. Mason Sailors.

Melissa's voice quickly brought me back to reality. "I've chosen the cucumber quiche for the last appetizer!" She shouted.

I was standing in the middle of the catering salon, still in a daze.

I shook my head and jumped into consultant mode. "That's wonderful!" I said with my hands still shaking. I had to get out of there. I looked at the watch on my wrist pretending as if I had somewhere else to be.

"Well would you look at the time!" I said while walking towards the door.

"Leaving Ash?" Melissa said, surprised that I gathered my things so quickly.

"Yes, I have a meeting with a groom and groom!" I called out. I wasn't completely lying, I did have a consultation with a groom who was planning to marry the love of his life in New York, but the meeting wasn't for another three hours. I simply needed the excuse to get out of the shock of seeing my ex fiancé after all these years. Making matters worse, he was happy. He wasn't fat, he looked great. He wasn't a bum, he obviously had a successful career that kept him away from his fiancé. The part that really got me was that he was in love. He was in love, and *I* was planning his wedding. Granted, I did like someone, but I was nowhere near planning the rest of my life with him yet. I grunted. Some karma. As a passed the mirror towards the entrance to the shop, I checked my makeup to make sure that it was still in-tact. If anything, I could at least say that I looked good. I gasped as I saw a particle of the piece of shrimp I had earlier still hanging on the side corners of my mouth. I angrily looked back at Melissa and

Mason-who couldn't keep their eyes off of each other, and hurried out of the catering office with tears welling in my eyes. As I walked past the window to my car, I could see Mason staring towards my way.

****

Three hours later passed by quickly, and I was on my way to meet Michael and Thomas, two men who were planning to celebrate their nuptials since tying the knot in New York. I usually didn't plan just receptions, but I made an exception for this couple. I had only spoken to them on the phone, and their happy disposition was something that I really needed in my life, especially now. They wanted to meet at a bar, and I happily agreed, I could definitely use a drink-or five. Although the inside of me felt crumbled to pieces, my outer appearance shined as if I was the happiest woman on Earth. I wore a white linen pantsuit with my favorite nude sandals. My hair was pulled back into a ponytail which would allow me to throw back shots of vodka without having my hair in the way. I walked into the bar and immediately spotted the duo, Michael and Thomas who were both sitting at the bar laughing as if they were long lost best friends.

"Well if it isn't the happy couple!" I said to the two lovebirds.

Michael turned around and smiled. "Ashley, what a pleasure!"

I nodded my head. "No, the pleasure is all mine." The loud Top 40 music played in the background, allowing me to relax and forget about today's- or should I say *this week's* events. The clouds coming from the bar's fog machine gave me an exhilarated feeling and crept down the spine of my back.

"Let's talk wedding!" I shouted over the loud music. It was still a little early in the evening, so the bar hadn't gotten too full. Still, the atmosphere was different from what I had experienced in a long time.

"Want to know why we brought you here?" Michael said as he motioned the bartender towards him.

"I was confused. No, why?" I said.

Thomas got up and started dancing. "This is where we want to celebrate our marriage!"

I looked around me. In a *bar*?

Michael looked into Thomas's eyes. He then turned to me and said, "This is where we first met. We want you to transform this place into a wedding wonderland. We want it to be special. Can you do that?"

I looked around the bar. Hell yeah, I could do it. That was my job.

"Nothing is impossible." I said with a smile.

Michael picked up a cocktail glass and handed it to me. "That's all we needed to know. You're hired!"

I took a sip of the pink cocktail. It was strong, but good. I winced at how the cocktail burned as it slid down my throat. It probably wasn't the most professional thing to do, drink in front of a client, but I needed the release. The world wasn't real at the moment, so I didn't have high expectations for myself.

"Great! I'm so excited to work with you gentlemen!"

"Likewise." Michael said. "Bartender! Another round for our new wedding planner, please." Michael smiled as he put a napkin in front of me to prepare me for the next drink.

"Meeting next Saturday to discuss the deets?" Michael said as he and Thomas got up to leave.

"Next Saturday it is." I said.

I smiled nervously as the bartender handed me another cocktail. I hadn't even finished the first. I quickly slurped the first drink down and started on the other. I waved to Michael and Thomas and decided to stay for another round. I was going to try my hardest to forget about seeing Mason once again. After two more drinks, I had come up with my conclusion. I was going to quit working for Melissa and focus on Michael and Thomas. I just couldn't deal with seeing Mason. Who plans their ex's wedding? Not me.

I felt a slight touch on my shoulder. I wasn't sure if it was because I was drunk or this person's hands were made of silk, but their touch felt good. I turned around and saw a fizzled version of Brandon smiling down at me.

"Busy day? I hadn't heard from you in a while." He said.

The words coming out of my mouth the next moment would have gotten me into a lot of trouble with the police had I driven home immediately.

"Yeah-I, I….yeah. Been busy."

I was drunk, but I could still notice that Brandon looked amazingly sexy that night. He wore a black button up shirt with matching slacks, smelling like expensive cologne. I fixed myself as quickly as I could to at least appear decent, and then stumbled out of my chair.

"Whoa," Brandon held me up to keep me from falling to the ground. "Do you even drink?" He looked at me confused.

"I do today," I said, not willing to reprise that day's events.

"Let's go home." Brandon held my hand to lead me to the door. I was drunk, but I wanted to know whose home he had in mind.

"My home?" I said as I stumbled towards the door with him.

"Uh, yeah, I meant, I am going to make sure you get home safely. Okay babe?"

He just called me babe. I liked it. I needed it.

"Yeah, sure." I said to Brandon as he guided me towards the exit.

****

The next morning I woke up in a daze. Of course, I was hung over, bad. I looked over to my side and Brandon was nowhere to be found. He had done just as he said and dropped me off at home safely. As I tried to recall the events from the day before, I heard the TV softly whispering from my living room. Brandon was laid out on my sofa, sound asleep. Turns out, he didn't go home. I tiptoed past him towards the kitchen. I wanted to make him a breakfast to express my gratitude.

A little while later, the smell of pancakes, bacon and eggs permeated the entire apartment. The aromas must have awaken Brandon, as he appeared with his hands in the air.

"Score, she's making me breakfast!" He said.

I put a spoonful of eggs on a plate and turned towards him. "Indeed I am." I said.

Brandon looked me up and down. I had changed into my black yoga pants and tank top after waking up. Brandon could notice every curve of my body. I noticed him looking and playfully put my hands over his eyes. "No peeking!" I said as I slapped him playfully. Things turned hot after he looked me in the eyes, his brown eyes instantly making me moan. Maybe he could help me forget about seeing Mason. I slammed the plate down on the table and softly brought his head towards mine. He kissed my lips, and I felt a wave of pleasure soaring through my body. His hands began to touch every inch of my body, making me moan softly. Sure, I was going a little too fast, but my mind wasn't thinking straight after seeing Mason.

Brandon stopped what he was doing. "Do you want me to stop?" he asked. I let my actions give him the answer as I brought him back towards me. His touch felt so amazing. Brandon picked me up and softly placed me on the counter. Our kisses turned from soft into rough and passionate. Our heavy breathing told each other that we both enjoyed what was happening, and it was nowhere near like the first time. I felt my soft spot become slippery with passion as he pulled down my tight black yoga pants. "Mmmm Brandon," I said as he slipped a finger inside of me. It felt so good. Randy was right, Mr. Purp couldn't do what the real thing could do. Brandon picked up the pace as he thrust his finger deep inside of me.

"Tell me what you want." He said.

"I want you inside of me." I said.

Brandon followed my orders and slowly pulled down his boxers, releasing his very stiff member. I was overcome with erotic pleasure. He pulled me to the edge of the counter and slipped inside of me. "Mmmm" I said as he slid in and out. Brandon could tell I loved it, he then sped up slightly, making me moan a little louder. "Brandon!" I shouted. Brandon's soft grunts told me that he was enjoying it too. I could feel a wave of ecstasy come across me-something another man had not given me in a long time. My soft spot began contracting intensely. Brandon held me close and thrust me with a gentle roughness that felt so good. "Ohhhhhh!!!" I shouted as I burst with pleasure. "Oh yeah, baby!" Brandon said as he sped his thrusts. We both climaxed at the same time. I looked up at Brandon-and gasped as I saw his face, all I could see was Mason. *Stop it.* I told myself. I closed my eyes and kissed Brandon on the lips, hoping that Mason's face would go away.

"You okay baby?" I opened my eyes and found Brandon staring at me passionately.

"I'm perfect." I said as I kissed Brandon on his forehead. I cursed myself for thinking about Mason while I was with Brandon-who had just given me the orgasm of a lifetime.

"Yes, you are perfect." Brandon said as he held my hand. I looked towards the window-the bright morning sun had just peaked. Brandon looked at me with a smile on his face.

"I have a question." he said.

"Sure babe, what's up?" I asked.

"Are you my girl?" Brandon asked.

I thought it was so cute how he asked me to be his girlfriend. I felt like I was in high school all over again. I kissed his smooth chiseled chest before answering.

"I'm your girl." I said.

"So as your boyfriend, I think I should have a key now. You know, for safety purposes." Brandon said. I smacked my lips and rolled my eyes at my new guy's request. He sure did know how to push it. I thought to myself that we were going a little too fast, but I needed something to take my mind off of Mason and I was positive that giving Brandon a chance would help.

"Okay, we will try it for one week. You aren't staying over all the time. Emergencies *only*. Got it?" I said as I held back laughs.

Brandon didn't reply, he simply held me closer to him, acknowledging my words. Just like that, I had a boyfriend.

As Brandon held me, I wondered if Mason made love to Melissa that morning too-and if he did, I wondered if he thought of me, even after all these years.

****

Later that morning, I walked into work with a pep in my step. You know, the pep that you get in your step after you just had amazing sex. Nothing could stop me, I was feeling great. I looked around for Randy and couldn't find him. I ignored his absence and floated into my office, looking forward to a productive day. My phone vibrated, and I smiled as I picked up my phone. It was from Brandon.

Today was amazing. It read.

I thought about this morning's events and felt a tingle in my forbidden spot.

Indeed it was. :-) I replied.

I couldn't help but feel slightly guilty for having Mason cross my mind. Brandon was an amazing guy-even with that chokehold kiss from the first date. I liked him. Or did I?

My mind began to race with so many thoughts. Seeing Mason completely threw me off guard. What are the chances that your college fiancé pops up into your life years later? Even worse, what are the odds that you plan their actual *wedding?* I started to think of states I could relocate to when Randy knocked on my door. I shook myself out of my daydreaming and greeted my best friend.

"Hey, stranger," I said to him smiling.

Randy squinted his eyes and clasped his hands.

"Yes, Finally!" he danced around my office.

"Finally what?" I said, confused. I hoped Brandon didn't call his cousin-and my best friend to tell him about earlier that morning. That would have been *weird.*

Randy took a break from his dancing. "I can see it all in your face, you got some, and it wasn't Mr. Purp who gave it to you."

"How am I wearing it on my face?" I said.

"Well, not exactly your face, but your neck. You ever heard of concealer?" Randy teased.

I covered my neck in embarrassment, remembering Brandon softly sucking on my neck during our lovemaking session. I was in such a rush, that I forgot to check for evidence before heading to work.

"Oh." I blushed.

Randy waved his hand in the air. "It's okay, you needed it."

"Hell yeah I needed it." I said motioning Randy to come closer. "Do you remember Mason?"

Randy's wide brown eyes turned into slits as he recalled my ex fiancé from college.

"Yeah, I remember that asshole. Had you depressed for weeks!"

I frowned. "Uh, yeah." It was more like years, but I didn't tell Randy that.

Randy laughed. "Did he finally get hit by a bus like you wanted?"

I looked up to the ceiling, still not being able to believe what I saw in the catering shop that day.

"Well, if the bus hit him and brought his ass back to L.A., yeah, sure."

Randy looked at me, confused.

"He's in L.A." I repeated.

"Oh okay, where did you see him, at *Sammies*?" Randy said, referencing my favorite restaurant.

My mind drew a blank. "No."

"Okay?" Randy had one eyebrow raised, looking for an answer.

"I'm planning his damn wedding!" I said.

"What?! Mason is gay?! I knew it." Randy said, thinking that Mason was either Michael or Thomas.

I put my finger in the air, correcting him. "No, he's Melissa's fiancé."

Randy gasped. The only word that could come out of his mouth matched what I was feeling since I saw him.

"Damn."

I dropped my head to the ground. "I know. Should I quit?"

"Hell no-well, yes! Okay, I don't know." Randy said.

Well there went the one justification I needed to quit.

"Does Melissa know?" he said.

I shook my head. "I have no idea. I'm thinking no, she hasn't even called and said anything."

"This is some messed up shit." Randy said.

I laughed. I'm sure it wasn't very often a heartbroken wedding consultant planned her ex's wedding by chance.

"I know Ran."

"Randolph!" Our conversation was cut short by the sound of Donald's annoying ass voice.

Randy turned his head to acknowledge Don.

"I gotta go Ash. Talk later." Randy said, uneasy. He then rushed off to Don's office and closed the door behind him.

I wondered what they were talking about as my phone vibrated. It was Melissa.

Shit.

I answered my phone in the most professional way I could. I didn't want to seem shaken.

Melissa's voice projected through the other line. She seemed to be in a busy location.

"Hey girl!" she shouted over many muffled voices.

"Hey!" I said, waiting for her to drop the bomb and tell me that my cover was blown.

"What are you doing tonight? Can you do dinner? It was Bubba's idea."

I grew nervous and couldn't stop myself as I said,

"Well, what does Bubba want?"

The other end of the line grew quiet, as if Melissa was trying to comprehend why I would say something so rude.

"He wants to get to know the wedding planner better." She said.

Oh trust me. He knows all about me. I thought to myself.

Obviously she didn't know. Or, she knew and was going to call me out on it at dinner. Either way, I was screwed. I figured dinner that night would be my way to politely bow out of the role as Melissa's wedding planner.

"Sure." I said, reluctantly of course.

"Great!" Meet at The *Plaza* at 7, it's Bubba's treat!"

As I hung up the phone, I squinted my eyes, again not believing this shit was happening to me.

I quickly grabbed my things, and headed to leave work and get something at the clothing boutique downtown. Of course, I had to look my best for 'Bubba's Dinner'. Randy appeared out of Don's office, headed towards me as if he had something to say. I didn't care, I was on a mission so I simply walked past him waving goodbye.

I had to make Mason see what he was missing.

****

As I walked into The *Plaza* restaurant, my head was spinning so much that I had to work to keep my balance. The jazz playing in the background helped calm me down slightly, but I couldn't ignore the crazy feelings going through my head. I noticed Melissa and Mason sitting at the table, whispering sweet nothings in each other's ears. They looked so happy. I waddled towards the table, attempting to pick my face off the floor at the same time. Melissa noticed me and smiled cheerfully as she pulled away from Mason.

"You're here!" she said.

Yep I was here, and I was tempted to turn around and go back home.

"Sit!" Melissa said, pointing me towards the chair in front of Mason.

I sat down, nervously smiling. I wondered if they could see my hands shaking as I picked up the menu.

Melissa sipped from her martini glass. "So, now that the two of you are acquainted, everything is complete! This is going to be my best wedding ever."

Mason playfully hit Melissa on the arm. "It should be your *only* wedding ever." He joked. I quietly snickered at the two lovebirds. I wasn't going to sit and witness this shit.

"I'm going to excuse myself to the ladies room." I said as I abruptly rose from my chair. This was beginning to be too much. Mason stared at me dead in the eyes as I motioned away from the table.

I entered the restroom and frowned when I noticed that there was only one mirror. There was a young lady standing by the mirror, picking at her face as if she was freshening up for a date. I didn't care what she was doing, she had to go. I caught eyes with her and squinted my eyes, purposefully intimidating her. She quickly closed her makeup compact and shuffled past me, giving me the opportunity to take her place in front of the mirror. Tears slowly trailed down my face as I thought about the memories Mason and I once shared. There I was, planning his entrance into a new life. I felt hurt and confused. I wondered what Melissa had that was so special. I sighed and realized that this was my job, and I had to do it. I wiped my tears and gave myself one final glance in the mirror.

"I can do this." I said to myself.

I could do this. I walked out of the restroom with my head held high, ready to take on anything.

My confidence shattered to pieces as I bumped into Mason walking back towards the table. The secluded hallway gave us privacy, so when he spoke to me, his loud tone of voice probably went unnoticed by others.

"Ash." He said.

I squinted my eyes. "Don't call me Ash."

Mason grabbed my arm and pulled me closer to him as if he were going to give me a kiss.

"Quit." He said quietly.

I rolled my eyes at his sudden request. I pulled my arm away from his grasp.

"You know what Mason, screw you. You still want everything your way I see. I wonder if Melissa knows that."

Mason positioned himself as if he were uncomfortable and spoke through gritted teeth.

"You cannot plan this wedding." He said.

I poked my head out of the hallway to see if Melissa had noticed our absence. She was sitting at the table, on her cell phone.

"Too late for that Mason," I said. "If you were actually interested in the wedding plans, you would have known who the hell her wedding planner was."

Mason appeared untouched. I hated how his nonchalant attitude could still affect me.

"I'm not giving you a damn choice. You quit. Now." He said.

I looked at him. He still had the ability to turn from sweet to a complete asshole.

"No." I said.

A part of me didn't actually know why I denied Mason's request. Was it because I was loyal to Melissa? Or did I just want to be close to Mason? I was driving myself crazy.

I fixed my dress and smiled. "See you at the table." I said.

Mason grunted and headed to the men's room.

I approached the dinner table, smiling as I noticed how gorgeous Melissa looked under the dim lights. She was going to make a beautiful bride.

Melissa smiled. "Did you get stuck in the toilet?" she joked.

No, but I hope your fiancé does. I thought to myself. It was corny, but it helped.

I laughed. "Not at all! Those luxury toilets are quite huge though."

Melissa chuckled and took a sip of her drink.

"I'm glad you finally met Bubba." She said.

"Me too." I hope she couldn't hint the sarcasm in my tone, because it was definitely there.

Melissa put her head down. "I was thinking that maybe if he met you, he would be more interested in the wedding planning you know?"

I contemplated why my presence would suddenly pique Mason's interest in the wedding planning.

"How so?" I replied, curious.

Melissa didn't reply. She ignored me and glared at Mason as he approached the table from the men's room. I scoffed as he sat down. As soon as Mason arrived, so did the food. I eyed the plate in front of me, afraid to touch it. I didn't want anything stuck on the side of my mouth like last time, but it looked delicious. Melissa smiled and held up her half empty martini glass. For such an elegant woman, she could probably drink a college freshman under the table.

"A toast." She said.

I quickly glanced at Mason who appeared calm and uneasy at the same time. I rolled my eyes and held up my glass. Mason followed suit and we toasted glasses as Melissa said, "To a perfect wedding."

I sat in the chair smiling while truly dying inside. *Right. Her perfect wedding. My screwed up life.*

****

The alarm woke me up right on time, 6am the next morning. I jumped out of bed immediately. Today was Rec Day at work, and I'd be damned if I didn't get the recognition I deserved. Even with the wedding planning business, I put a lot into Briggs Solutions Incorporated. With everything that happened in the past week or so, a Rec Day would do all of the employees some good. I picked up my phone and texted Randy.

"Rec Day!"

Randy liked Rec Day as well, so I knew he'd be excited. I was surprised when ten minutes passed by with no reply from Randy. I cocked my head to the side in curiosity, he was usually quick with text messages, especially from me. As I sat the phone on my nightstand, I was startled when I heard my doorbell ring. I slowly walked to the door, mostly because I'm not used to having guests in my house, I usually go to theirs. If I went slowly enough, they would go away. This person at the door was different and continued to ring the doorbell until I let them in. I peeked out of my door and was surprised to see that it was Melissa at the door.

Oh shit.

I opened the door reluctantly, thinking that she has finally found me out. Her smile assured me that nothing was wrong.

"Hey girl!" Melissa said as she hugged me, pushing her way through the door. I wondered if she realized what time it was.

"Hey." I replied. I wasn't sure what her motives were for stopping by my house. I looked at the outfit she was wearing, she sure did look nice. Her floral print dress matched the cardigan she wore on her shoulders. I laughed to myself, she really did look like someone's wife.

"It's bridal shower time!" She said as she plopped on my couch.

"How wonderful!" I said. I walked toward my room to get dressed, hoping that would give her the hint to leave. I liked Melissa, but now that Mason was in the picture, things were just too weird.

Melissa put her head down.

"Actually, that's not why I'm here." She said.

I became scared. I hated to see her so upset, but I actually wanted to make sure she didn't find out about Mason and I. In reality, she was more than a client, she was also a friend. I sat down next to her and put my hand on her shoulder.

"What's wrong Melissa?" I inched closer to her to make her more comfortable.

"It's Mason."

My heart stopped. Had Mason told her? That was it. I had to say something. I held my breath for a moment to find the words.

"You know, if Mason hasn't already told you-" I started. Before I could finish my sentence, Melissa was crying and waving her hands all over the place.

"His mom hates me!" She said.

I smiled to myself. She didn't know.

Relieved, I patted her back with concern.

"Oh no! What happened?"

"She keeps asking him if he is sure he wants to get married. That bitch!" Melissa squinted her eyes as she described her future mother in law.

Then it hit me who she was talking about. Miss Daphine, Mason's mom. I smiled as I remembered the times we shared together and how much we bonded over the years Mason and I were together. I then frowned as I thought about how she dumped me as fast as Mason did. Once I was out of his life, I was out of hers.

"I'm sure she isn't that bad!" I assured her. I wondered what kind of person Miss Daphine thought Melissa was, especially since Melissa was the sweetest woman in the world to me. Many of my brides were complete bitches for no reason. Melissa was different. She was kind. I adjusted my position on the couch. I didn't want Melissa to see the smile I had on my face as she talked about Mason's mother.

I was very excited as I opened the package from Miss Daphine. Mason always sent me things, but receiving something from his mother made me feel really great. In the package were beautiful rose stationary sets and a letter. I opened the letter and smiled as I read the words on the page. "You are such a blessing to Mason, I am glad he has someone like you in his life." It was amazing that his mother thought to write such beautiful things about me. I put the letter in my letter box and promised myself that I would keep it forever.

"Can you talk to him?" Melissa brought me out of my thoughts.

"Sure! Wait-what?" I couldn't believe I was agreeing to meet with Mason-alone.

I could tell Melissa was growing slightly irritated by the way she rolled her eyes as she began the next sentence.

"One of your duties as wedding planner is to mediate bridal party issues. Right?" She said.

I looked to the ceiling. I didn't recall listing mediating family disputes as one of my services.

"And, were friends, right? Do it as my friend." Melissa looked at me with that beautiful smile of hers. I couldn't resist.

"I don't see why not." I said.

"What do you want me to say?" I looked at Melissa with questionable eyes. I was hoping she wouldn't ask me to speak to Miss Daphine herself. That would be completely awkward.

Melissa scoffed. "Tell him to tell his momma that she is a psycho bitc-"

"You mean, tell her that your feelings are hurt?" I cut her off, wanting to remain as professional as possible. Melissa gave me a confused look and agreed.

"Yeah, that works too I guess." She said.

I smiled. I wasn't sure why, but I seemed to be happy to get Mason alone. I would keep it strictly professional, of course.

"I need you to do it immediately." Melissa pleaded. "I'm not sure how much more I can take! He needs to stand up to her."

I looked to the ground, not sure why I was so excited to talk to Mason. He didn't care about me, he dropped off of the Earth almost ten years ago. It shouldn't have mattered to me, but it did.

Melissa gave me a hug and quickly ran to the door.

"Thanks Ash, I'll have Bubba give you a call. Okay?"

I kept myself from looking uneasy, this was it.

"Okay." I said.

Melissa mouthed the words "Thank You" and closed the door behind her. I almost had the courage to tell her, but I couldn't. I started to think about how selfish it was not to tell her. The best part of me cared about hurting her feelings. A part of me didn't care. In a way, I felt liked she *owed* me. Mason owed me. Then I thought about the mistake I was making. Not only could this ruin my friendship with Melissa, it could also ruin the reputation of Bella Bride. I walked to the bathroom to continue getting dressed for work. I was digging myself into a big pile of shit, and the worst part was, I knew what I was doing.

****

"And the award for Most Creative goes to Ashley!" I smiled as the room clapped their hands to congratulate my award. Rec Day was the one day every associate at Briggs Solutions felt important. I walked up to receive the award and smiled like a kid about to receive candy. Along with the award came a $500 bonus and there were lots of things I could do with the money. I looked to the audience and saw Randy. He didn't look happy. The ceremony was coming to a close, I was the last person to receive an award. The reception following the ceremony couldn't come fast enough, I was really hungry. As I entered the reception area, I spotted Randy next to the chicken wing platter eating off of a red plate. I was surprised that he did not text me all day, and that he looked upset during the ceremony. Randy received an award for "Most Innovative", so it wasn't Rec Day that made him upset. I smiled cheerfully as I approached my best friend.

"Hey, you!" I said, poking Randy as I approached him from behind.

Randy turned around and squinted his eyes when he noticed it was me.

"Oh, hey." He said.

I looked at him, confused. I wondered why he was acting so weird. So, I just came out and asked.

"Why the hell are you acting so weird?" I said.

Randy looked to the ground. "It's nothing."

I could see that Randy was fighting to say something. When he finally said it, it dawned on me why he was acting so weird.

"Are you applying for the position?" He asked.

I cocked my neck back in surprise. That was why he was acting weird?

"I don't know, are you?" I questioned him.

Randy shook his head. "Well, I don't know."

I knew he wanted it. Randy and I always worked together, and I'm sure he felt that it was time to get his accolades. Not convinced with his answer, I asked him again.

"Are you sure?"

"Don told me that I was the right man for the job." Randy said.

I wondered why in the hell Don would even tell us about the position in the same room. We would have found out anyway, but I think Don did that out of spite, just to be an asshole.

I grabbed a cookie and put it on my plate. Once I realized it was oatmeal raisin, I surveyed the platter and picked up a chocolate chip cookie instead.

"Well, if he thinks you are the right man for the job, I don't see why you shouldn't have it." I said as I bit out of my cookie. Randy was my best friend. I wasn't trying to lose a friend over a job. Plus, I already had so much going on with Bella Bridal, I felt that I could take a loss.

I sighed. "Ran, if you want this job, go for it, okay?"

Randy smiled. "Okay."

We exchanged awkward glances as I felt my phone vibrate. It was a text from an unknown number.

It's Mason. Melissa said you wanted to talk.

Melissa doesn't waste any time. I thought to myself. My hands were shaking as I texted him back. He still had the ability to change my entire mood.

I do. Meet me at Sammie's at 6.

As I hit send, I realized that 6pm was in a few hours. I didn't have time to go home and freshen up. Shit. I looked in the mirror and smiled as I noticed that I looked okay. My skirt business suit was tight in all the right places. I didn't want to admit it, but I was excited to see Mason.

As I neared *Sammie's* my heart was beating fast. I felt like I was about to have a heart attack. I was scared how Mason would react when he had the chance to finally be alone with me. Would he tell me he still love me? Would he apologize? I smiled to myself as I saw Mason sitting towards the back of the restaurant. He was his usual studious self, wearing a green polo and well-tailored pants. I had to stop myself from lusting over him-over another client's fiancée.

Then I thought to myself, he was mine first.

"Hello, Ashley." Mason acknowledged me without looking up from the screen of his cell phone.

"Mason."

I didn't want him to see how excited I was. I felt like a college sophomore all over again.

"What did she tell you?" Mason said.

I was surprised-if not disappointed that he didn't ask me how I was doing or anything. I raised an eyebrow at his rudeness.

"It's been almost ten years." I said. That was all I had the courage to cough up. Mason looked at me.

"Right. It's time you get over it. We were in college."

"But you left me cold!" I screamed at Mason, turning the heads of a few patrons within the restaurant. I stopped myself as the server approached the table, asking for our drinks.

"I'll have an iced tea, and she will have a water with lemon." Mason ordered.

I couldn't believe that after all these years, he still remembered that I only ordered water with lemon at restaurants. I smiled.

"You remembered."

Mason flicked his napkin and laughed. "Of course I do, your picky ass."

I laughed. It at least felt great that he remembered something about me. I guess he wasn't the selfish bastard I thought he was after all. The server soon returned with our drinks in hand.

Mason cleared his throat and was back on point. "We are here to talk about Melissa."

I nervously stirred my water with lemon. "Actually we aren't. We are here to talk about Miss Daphine." It felt so weird saying her name.

"My mother?" Mason scoffed. I chuckled, he was still the same mama's boy I knew from years ago. Even then, according to Mason, Miss Daphine could do no wrong.

"Melissa said had been very rude to her, on several occasions."

Mason sighed heavily. "I know my mom can sometimes be a tough case but Melissa shouldn't be discussing our issues with our wedding planner."

"I'm a little bit more than a wedding planner Mason, we are sort of becoming friends." I looked at Mason, wondering how he felt after I announced that his new fiancé and ex fiancé were now friends.

"Is that why you didn't quit? Because Melissa is such a good friend?" Mason looked at me as if I was hiding something.

"Yes." I said, trying to convince myself.

"Still a good liar I see." Mason said.

I thought back to the last time he called me a liar.

"It's over." The text message read. I didn't know what Mason meant, and I didn't know why he would do it over a text message. I was confused. "Is it someone else?" I asked. "No." Mason replied. I knew things weren't going great, but they weren't going horribly. I couldn't pinpoint it, but I knew that over the summer things had changed. We were in the middle of planning a wedding, venue set, dress ordered. He couldn't back out now. We were supposed to spend the rest of our lives together. "Mason, you can't do this!" I cried. "Yes, I can, I'm not happy. I'm moving to New Zealand like I told you I was. You are such a liar, and you don't know how to treat a man." My heart was racing. How could he do this to me? I looked at the text message again to make sure what was happening was real. My heart broke into pieces when I realized that everything was indeed real.

I forcefully put my cup on the table, causing the table to loudly shift. It was time that I voiced my anger. Not only did the situation make me upset, the flashback didn't help. "You know what, I didn't come here for this." I said as I pushed my plate to the middle of the table.

"Just tell me why you didn't quit. You had your chance the other night at dinner. Hell, you had your chance the day you first saw me at the catering place." Mason said. He stared at me, waiting for an answer.

"I don't know." I shook my head.

"You know." He said.

I did know, and it was completely selfish of me. I didn't even know why I was still there. A part of me just wanted an apology, another part of me wanted to have a piece of the happiness I had so many years ago. Even if was slightly fabricated.

"I should go." I said as I gathered my things.

Mason didn't say anything, he just stared. There I was, about to leave, without even doing what Melissa had told me to do. I was losing my way.

"I will talk to my mother." Mason said as I turned to the door.

Who was I kidding, I was beginning to think I was a little crazy. I had to let go.

"Okay." I whispered as I walked towards the door.

Mason didn't say goodbye as he picked up his cell phone. I left with my heart stuck in my throat. I had to quit.

****

I arrived at my apartment feeling defeated. I hadn't felt defeated in a long time. I was usually the strong one, I was the bitch. There I was with my head hanging down. There was no reason why I should have allowed someone to make me feel that way. Even though Mason once loved me, I shouldn't have expected him to love me forever. To Mason, I was out of sight, out of mind. After we broke up, we went our separate ways. I was confused once I opened my door, letting myself in without using a key. It didn't seem to be a break in, everything was still intact.

I still shouted just in case someone was there, they would leave.

"Who's there?" I shouted through the apartment.

"It's me baby!" I heard from the back room. It was Brandon, my new boyfriend. With all of the things going on, I forgot that we had agreed for him to have a key. Once I reminded myself, it made me happy that I would have someone to talk about my day with. Well, most of my day.

"Come here baby!" Brandon shouted. I was hungry, so I headed to the kitchen first.

"One second babe, let me grab this cookie!"

I grabbed the cookie, put it in my mouth and headed to the back room. I almost choked on it when I saw Brandon. There he was, in my bed, butt-naked with whipped cream covering his forbidden spot. In the background, I could hear a weird song playing that I'm sure he thought was romantic. It wasn't. I mentally slapped myself for giving this man a key so quickly.

"Come to Papa." Brandon said, patting my side of the bed.

I laughed, from the first date until tonight, this guy was seriously the corniest lover ever. I smiled as I stripped down to just my bra and panties. It was great to laugh.

Brandon hopped on me, forgetting that he had smothered whipped cream all over himself, because my body was soon covered with white speckles.

"Oops, that's not sexy." Brandon said as he jumped off of me.

I began to laugh. "No baby, I love it!" Sometimes I gave Brandon a hard time, but he tried, and I could appreciate that.

"Lick it off." I joked, ridiculing him for plastering me with the whipped cream from his body.

"You don't have to tell me twice." Brandon said as he inched towards me thigh to retrieve the dairy treat.

I moaned as he lovingly licked my inner thigh. It felt so good. I closed my eyes and slowly opened them, hoping I wouldn't see Mason's face appear like the last time we made love. As they opened, I closed them suddenly to prevent seeing what I didn't want to see. I slowly pushed Brandon off of me. "Not tonight, babe." I said as I gave him a kiss on the cheek. He was a great guy, and I didn't think it was fair to him to think about another man while Brandon was inside of me. Brandon raised himself off of the bed, confused. "I thought you were into it babe? I can get more whipped cream if you want me to!" He said as he grabbed the bottle of whipped cream off of the nightstand.

I shook my head. "No babe, you did great, but I'm just so tired. Let's go to sleep okay?"

Brandon raised an eyebrow and laid next to me. "You don't know how to handle it huh?" He said as he pushed me playfully. I looked at him and chuckled.

"Guess I don't! You can teach me, but not tonight. Got it?" I winked an eye at my boyfriend before turning off the lamp.

Brandon didn't say anything, he responded with a loud snore. I felt relieved that I wouldn't have to feel so bad about denying Brandon. Hopefully, it wouldn't last too much longer.

I was awakened the next morning by my phone sounding a text alert. Disoriented, I rolled over and checked my phone while trying to make sure I didn't wake Brandon. I gasped when I saw the text. It was from the same unknown number from the other day, which I translated as Mason's. I opened the text anxious to see what he wrote.

CAN WE MEET?

I was excited and confused at the same time. Why would Mason want to meet me? The other day didn't go so well, and I was heavily contemplating quitting-not only for Melissa's sake, but for my own. Feeling defeated, I texted back quickly. Mason knew how to get me going.

Why?

It took Mason a few moments to reply, but when he did, my heart stopped as I read the text.

I just need to see you.

Wow. Mason wanted to see me. I didn't know what to say, my first intention was to say no. My heart told me to say yes. Maybe Mason saying sorry would allow me to let go and quit while I still had time.

Okay.

Mason replied immediately.

Meet me at the pier. I hope you remember where that is. Btw, don't mention this to Melissa.

My heart skipped a beat. Would he apologize? Would he tell me that he loved me? I was very anxious to see what he had to say. I quickly texted him back, assuring him that meeting him was something that I really wanted to do.

Sounds good. See you there. 6 o clock, the pier.

Randy stepped into my office while my mind was adrift.

"Ash, we really need to talk."

I looked at the time. It was 5:15pm. I looked at my best friend and smiled. "How about brunch tomorrow? We can talk then." I said, blowing him off.

Randy frowned. "Ash-"

I patted Randy on the back as I walked out the door.

"Tomorrow okay? I'll tell you all about where I'm going then." I rushed out the door, not noticing the concern on Randy's face.

The only thing that was on my mind was six o clock. At the pier.

****

I arrived at the pier about 15 minutes early, anxious to see what Mason had to say in such a hurry. I straightened my posture as I spotted him walking towards me.

"Hey." He said as he approached me.

"Hi." I didn't know whether to be happy or scared. Was he going to try to get me to quit again? I stood there silently, waiting for an answer. I turned away from Mason, looking towards the water. The dolphins rising in and out of the water caused a slight smile to spread across my face.

"Do you remember this place?" Mason said as he turned the same direction I was looking into.

I did. It was the place we came to after our first date. The place I took him to where we engraved our names into the concrete when the pier was being rebuilt. I wondered to myself if the engraving was still there.

"I do." I said, nonchalant. I didn't want him to know that I remembered every memory we had together.

"I do too." Mason said.

I grunted. "Okay. Why did you bring me here Mason? Look, if you are trying to get me to quit again-"

Mason put his finger on my lip, telling me with his body language to hush.

"After we broke up, I used to come here all the time before I left L.A., to think about what we shared, what we lost." Mason said, looking towards the ground.

My eyes grew wide. All these years, Mason had thought about me too? I was completely surprised-and relieved. I didn't show him that.

I rolled my eyes. "And?"

"Our initials are still there. Right in the same spot." Mason said as he pointed to the direction we engraved our names in almost ten years ago.

I kept my attitude. "It's concrete. Of course it's not going anywhere."

Mason smiled. "Still got that little smart mouth I see."

I squinted my eyes. "Yeah, I do."

"Remember when you used to throw pennies here?" Mason said.

"I still do, when I'm stressed." I told Mason as I looked towards the sky. I imagined how many pennies I threw into the water over the years, because it seemed like I was always stressed.

"How did you and Melissa meet?" I asked. I dug a penny out of my pocket and threw it into the water. This conversation was stressing me out.

Mason laughed. "I met her in a nightclub, she was the worst dancer in the club, and I thought it was so cute."

I snickered as he clamored over his bride to be. I shouldn't have asked. I threw another penny into the water, hoping to ease my stress.

"Do you love her?" I asked.

"Of course I do." He said. By the look of his face, I couldn't tell whether he was being truthful or not. A part of me really didn't want to know.

"I never stopped thinking about you." Mason said, looking deeply into my eyes.

I wasn't impressed- or maybe I was. "Well, you were the one that left me, through a text."

Mason raised his voice, attempting to defend himself. "I was 22!"

"I was heartbroken!" I shouted back. We quieted down once we noticed that a few people at the pier were staring at us.

"There is just one thing I want." I said to Mason. It was something that I wanted for years, maybe it could help my heart heal.

"Are you going to quit?" Mason cut my thought process.

"I don't know." I said.

"Don't tell Melissa. Just keep it to yourself. She needs you." He said reluctantly.

I nodded. I could keep a secret, but not for too long.

"I have to tell her soon, Mason." I told him. In the back of my head, I wanted to bring up the fact that I wanted an apology from him. I was a little disappointed that he didn't do it.

"No, you don't. She will fire you, the wedding will go haywire, and then she will hate me." Mason laughed.

I smiled. "Okay, you got me!"

Mason and I exchanged glances and for a second, it felt like we had gone back in time as we stood in the same spot we stood when we were in love, years ago.

That moment ended as Mason glanced at his cell phone as it vibrated. From the uncomfortable look on his face, I could tell it was Melissa. Mason looked at me as if he were attempting to get approval from me to talk to his own fiancé.

"Answer it." I said.

Mason nodded and picked up the phone. I could hear Melissa's muffled voice on the other end, asking where Mason was.

Mason fed Melissa a lie so good, even I started to believe it. I shook my head in dismay. This wasn't going to end well if I didn't stop myself. Soon.

"Yeah babe, the meeting is over. I'm on my way. Love you too."

Mason looked my way and tilted his head.

"I have to go." He said.

He kissed my forehead and left me standing where I was-for another woman. I rolled my eyes. I felt like the insecure 21 year-old that was heartbroken after a broken engagement years ago. I didn't say anything as Mason walked off and watched as he got into his car and drove off in a hurry. After watching him disappear into the horizon, I turned towards the ocean and thought about what I was getting myself into.

****

It was hard for me to concentrate the next day at work. I didn't know what had transpired with Mason and I. Was that his way of saying he was still in love with me? I had no idea. I was completely confused. I thought to myself, ignoring the stack of papers piling on my desk. I had a lot of work to do, but my mind just couldn't stay focused. The happenings at Bella Bride took over my thoughts. Briggs Solutions didn't really run across my mind. Randy knocked on my door as I sat at my desk, deep in my thoughts.

"Hey, you." Randy said as he walked in, closing the door behind him.

"Hey!" I greeted Randy cheerfully.

"I've been meaning to talk to you about something." Randy said.

"What's up?" I inquired.

"I want to take the job." Randy said.

The room was silent for a moment. I hadn't even thought about the job issue. Ever since Mason stepped into the picture, I completely forgot about everything else. I shamed myself quietly for not handling business like I usually do.

"That's great Ran." I replied. I figured I had missed my chance, plus, I didn't want to lose a friend over a promotion. Randy deserved it.

Randy smiled. "Are you sure? I didn't want to cross you. I know how important Briggs Solutions is to you."

"It's obviously not *that* important, look at all the work I haven't done." I said, pointing to the mass of papers sitting atop of my desk.

Randy laughed. Randy was my friend since college, and I wanted to see him happy.

"You deserve it completely." I said to Randy as I approached him, patting on his back. "Now, start with doing all of this work on my desk, since you will be the boss and all." I joked.

Randy waved his hand. "Oh no, I'm the boss, I tell *you* what to do."

I chuckled and changed the subject.

"I saw Mason again."

A look of concern grew upon Randy's face. "Oh?"

"He gave me a kiss on the forehead, took me to the pier. We used to hang out there years ago." I said, replaying the night in my head. Even though the encounter was brief, it was wonderful.

"You need to quit, before you break that girl's heart." Randy said, referring to Melissa.

"I'm trying Ran!"

"Not hard enough." He said.

He was right. I could have been gone already. But I didn't quit. A part of me didn't want to break Melissa's heart, she was around 1 month way from the wedding. The other part of me didn't want to let Mason go. I didn't know whether I was being selfless or selfish. Either way, someone was going to get hurt. I had dibs on that person being me.

"Okay. I will take Melissa to dinner soon, and I will quit. Okay?" I assured Randy that I was going to do the right thing. Or maybe I was trying to assure myself.

"Sooner than later." Randy said.

I shook my head. "Yep, sooner than later."

As Randy and I stood coming to the conclusion that I was finally going to quit, the secretary knocked on my door with a bouquet of red roses in hand. I smiled as I thought of Brandon.

"These are gorgeous." The secretary said. "Someone loves you."

I shrieked. Brandon sure could pull out the whipped cream tonight. He was doing all the right things. As I held the vase in my hand, I almost dropped it to the floor as I read the card. It wasn't from Brandon.

"I remembered how you always liked roses. Enjoy. Mason."

Randy stood in front of me, looking confused. "Did the card say 'I've got herpes' or something? Why did you turn pale?"

I shoved the card in Randy's face without saying a word.

"Oh shit." He said.

"I've got to get rid of these." I said, finding a place to hide them. If Brandon ended up surprising me at work and saw the flowers, he would shit bricks.

"Or give them to me, I've got a date tonight and I want the girl to give me some ass. These will definitely do the trick." Randy said, eyeing the flowers.

I laughed and smacked my lips. "Ran, you are something else."

"Bet you are going to give Mason some ass. Married or not." Randy said.

"He's not married yet." I shot back.

"Yep. You are going to give him some." Randy sighed as he walked towards the door. I didn't know whether to laugh at Randy's comment or be offended. In my mind, to sleep with a man in a relationship was appalling.

"Just know what you are getting yourself into. Oh-and if you really don't want those flowers, drop them off at my house. Don't forget to take the note out." Randy said.

"I'm not giving you the flowers Ran." I said as I shooed him towards the door. As Randy left my office, my boss Donald, came in. Uninvited, of course.

"Flowers?" Don said, pointing at the red roses on my desk.

I hid the note behind my back. "My mother sent them."

Don raised an eyebrow, not believing what I said. "Your mom sure does love you."

"Uh, yeah. How can I help you Don?"

"We need to talk." Don said.

I figured that.

"Well?" I replied.

Don sat quietly before speaking. "It looks like that position is going to be open sooner than later."

"The manager position?"

"Yes."

"Okay. And?"

"I want you to do it." Don said.

I was confused, I thought that Don said the best man would get the job, and Randy said that he wanted it. I was going to simply let Randy have it.

Don continued. "In fact, you *have* to take the position, because I'm cancelling yours."

I frowned. Was that Don's way of pitting Randy and I against each other?

I stuttered as I spoke. This was not going to be good.

"I-I-I thought you wanted either of us to have it? Randy has expressed interest in the job."

"I don't care." Don said. "I want you. First thing I want you to do is fire Randy."

"Donald! What? What the hell is going on?" I said loudly. Things were turning for the worse.

"He's smart-mouthed, and his work isn't all that good. Since Mr. Briggs died, we need to downsize anyway. That is why I am getting rid of Randy, cancelling your position, and putting you as manager. Why are you so upset? You win!"

"Randy is my best friend."

"And this is the advertising world. Do you like what you do?" Donald said, speaking with a serious tone.

"I do."

"Prove it. You have two weeks." Don walked out of the door without receiving my response. I sat at my desk, thinking if I would rather lose my job than to have Randy lose his. While I sat contemplating, Randy walked into my office with a smile on his face.

"I'm ready to officially apply! What did Don say?" he said, beaming.

I was at a loss for words. I couldn't tell him at that moment. Damn. There I was again, keeping another secret for my own sake, not thinking of how it would affect those around me. I sat in my chair, not saying a word. He noticed that my disposition was slightly different than before Don entered the room. I'm sure he took my silence as offensive.

"Is everything okay?" he said.

"Yeah, everything is fine." I lied.

"You want the job don't you Ash?" Randy said.

"No, that's not it at all."

"So then, what's up?"

Silence.

"You should be happy for me Ash. I thought you wanted me to do this!"

I looked up at Randy, not knowing what to say. How was I supposed to tell my best friend that our boss wanted him fired?

"I am happy for you Ran. You know that."

Randy frowned and stared at the ground. "Guess we shall see if you really are. See you later." Randy turned towards the door and walked out without our usual laughs. I was at a loss for what to do. If I don't fire him, I lose my job. If I fire him, I have my job, a better job at that, but I lose my best friend. It seemed like the world was crashing down on me. I sighed heavily as I felt my phone vibrate. It was Mason. Again.

"Hope you got the surprise! Just wanted to apologize for leaving so quickly yesterday."

My smile quickly turned upside down once I realized what I was doing. Mason could apologize for leaving his "meeting" with me, but was yet to apologize for breaking my heart. I thought that was what he brought me to the pier for anyway. That's all I wanted, an apology. Then, I figured I would be able to move on. I texted him back, a little less friendly than before.

"Yesterday you didn't give me what I wanted."

I probably should I checked the context of my text, because his reply was:

"A kiss?"

"No, an apology." I replied. That was all I wanted. I think.

I waited a few minutes, Mason didn't text back at the same speed he did before my request. I figured Melissa or someone came and took his attention away. Or, he was just being an asshole. I sighed heavily. Why did all the bad and confusing things happen to me? Why couldn't I just *get* a promotion, why did I have to fire my best friend in order to make it to the top? And better yet, why couldn't I keep my thoughts off of someone else's man? Well, in my defense, he was mine first. I got up to leave the office for the day, not wanting to know what tomorrow would bring.

****

I walked into my apartment, hoping to see Brandon waiting for me, even if he had one of those whipped cream fiascos planned. I looked around the house and was disappointed to find that he wasn't there. I figured I hurt his feelings from the other day. I made sure I left the flowers back at the office just in case he did show. I could lie to Donald about where the roses came from, but Brandon wouldn't be so easy. I texted my boyfriend to find out where he was. A part of me was hoping to see that Mason had replied from my text earlier, but he hadn't. I rolled my eyes as I waited for Brandon to reply, informing me of his whereabouts.

"I'm home."

"Come here, I've got whipped cream and strawberries!" I replied.

"How about another day?" Brandon said.

I wondered why he didn't want to see me.

"Okay". Was the only word I could text back. I had a lot on my mind, I didn't want to take my worry out on Brandon anyway. I figured a night apart wouldn't do any harm. I began to walk to the kitchen as my phone vibrated. I gasped with happiness when I noticed Mason's name flash across the screen. I hurriedly opened the text.

"Hey, are you busy?"

I began to contemplate on what I should say to Mason. Sure, I used to be in love with him, and when I'm around him, it's like he stole my heart all over again. But, I knew it wasn't right. I was at risk with damaging the reputation of Bella Bride if word got out that I was hanging out with my client's fiancé. I immediately threw the phone down and ignored his text. I couldn't go through this again, who knows what could happen. When my phone vibrated again, I checked my phone, not expecting it to be Mason. It was.

"You there?"

I tried.

I replied to his message quickly, hoping that he didn't step away from the phone.

"I'm here. What's up?"

"Can we meet again?" Mason texted.

I replied yes. I didn't need to see him, but I wanted to. There was something about Mason that turned me on. I couldn't shake it, even after all of these years. I went to my closet, put on a simple dress that didn't scream "I want you." I didn't want to send the wrong message. Or at least I thought I didn't. As I looked into the mirror, I began to think about another dress from my past.

I walked into the bridal shop and was greeted by the saleswoman, beaming. Holding back tears, I asked to receive my wedding dress. "And you are?" She asked me. I looked at her in disbelief, for she told me that she would always remember my smiling face from the day I found my wedding dress. I stuttered, "My name is Ashley Weeks". After finally recognizing who I was, she smiled.

"Oh! It's you!" She gave me a knowing look as if I looked different. We both knew that I didn't look the same. My hair was ragged, I had glasses on and my eyes were bloodshot red from crying the entire drive to the shop. The look I gave her was "Listen bitch, just give me my dress" but I proceeded to just smile quietly and wait as she rushed to the back to retrieve my gown. As she scattered through the closet to locate my dress, my eyes were once again welling up with tears. I couldn't take it. I didn't want to see it. It took me two months to come and get the dress in the first place. I had finally mustered up the strength to get it and as I sat in that shop I started to think I made a mistake. Just around six months before, I was prancing around in the dress with everyone clamoring over how beautiful I looked. She gracefully re-entered the room-pink gown bag in hand. "How's the wedding planning going anyway?" She asked. I choked. "Umm….there is no wedding." I replied. I could have easily just told her things were going great, but I felt the need to say it, call me crazy. Nodding as if I had just confirmed her thoughts, she said "It was for the best."

She was right. It was for the best. I needed to see him. I gathered my things and headed out the door to meet Mason.

I approached Mason and saw him looking as handsome as can be. I smiled and headed towards him. I hadn't seen or heard from Melissa in days, I made a note to call her the next morning. I mean, after all, I was her wedding planner. I stopped myself and noticed that since I didn't look sexy, I needed to overcompensate. I started to strut towards him, not noticing the soda can sitting below my feet. I gasped as my foot struck the soda can and I fell backwards. Great.

"Are you okay?" Mason said, running to my rescue.

I got up and dusted myself off. I sighed as I saw a big brown spot resting on top of my dress.

"I'm fine." I said, embarrassed.

Mason laughed. "I hope you aren't embarrassed, you used to fart around me. Remember?"

I looked down at the spot on my dress and answered Mason. "That was years ago."

"And I'm sure you still fart." Mason replied, chuckling.

I cut to the chase. He needed to stop bringing me to the pier for no reason.

"Listen, what is this about? We already met yesterday." I said.

"I'm not over you." Mason blurted.

He wasn't over me. After all these years, he wasn't over me. Yet, he is marrying someone else. How convenient. I tried to remain untouched when in reality, I was jumping in circles.

"And?" I said.

Mason looked at me with love. "There is no and. I'm about to marry Melissa and you are the wedding planner. I had no idea that I wasn't over you, until the day I saw you at the café. And yes, I noticed the shrimp you had on the side of your mouth."

I laughed at how Mason could still pay attention to the little things.

"Well *Bubba,* there is nothing you can do about it." I said, poking fun at Mason's newfound nickname.

"Why does she call you Bubba anyway?" I asked. Bubba didn't fit him at all.

Mason chuckled with conceit. "Now, we both know, I may not be fat, but other things are." He said, jokingly pointing towards his private parts.

"Yuck! I don't want to hear that!" I said covering my eyes. When I took my hands off of my eyes, I noticed that Mason now stood a couple inches closer toward me. He was so close I could feel the warmth of his breath. His hands held the side of my arm, sending tingles down my spine. Overcome with guilt, I pulled myself away from his grasp.

"What are you doing?" I asked Mason.

Mason stared at me, as if I was the one he was supposed to marry next month. I began to feel uncomfortable.

"Let's stop." I said.

Mason looked at me, confused. "Stop what? I haven't even kissed you yet."

Yet? There was no absolute way I would kiss Mason. There was no way I could do anything to hurt Melissa. Not only was she a client, but she was a friend.

"Are you okay?" Mason asked as I looked out to the sky, not knowing what to do.

I smacked my lips. "Well, I tripped trying to be sexy for you, oh-and I don't want to kiss you. That's what wrong."

"Well, let's try." Mason said, puckering his lips out.

I laughed.

"We both know this isn't right. I had no idea you even felt this way about me still."

"What way?" Mason asked.

"You know, romantic!" I blurted. There was no way he was still playing mind games 10 years out of college.

"I don't know what it is." Mason said.

"Maybe you are just trying to relive what happened in the past." I said, attempting to blot the spot out of my dress.

"Let's find out." Mason looked at me with love in his eyes.

"What do you mean?" I said.

Mason rubbed my arm softly. "I want to make love to you tonight."

"Mason, no." I said as I stepped away from him. This couldn't be happening. To think all this time, this was something that I thought I wanted.

"Are you sure?" Mason asked.

I shook my head. "I'm sure. Let's go."

"Alright, let's go." Mason said as he turned towards the parking lot. We both walked to the lot quietly, not knowing what to say. As soon as we approached my car, Mason escorted me to the door and opened it.

"Thank you." I said as he held out my car door.

I sat down in my seat and noticed that Mason hadn't said anything. He also didn't close the door to go to his car. I could feel the sexual tension rising within me as each second passed. Our words were replaced by silence and heavy breathing. I looked at Mason and saw the love I had for him so long ago. Without thinking, I jumped into his arms and our lips intertwined instantly. It felt amazing. Mason lifted my dress and slipped his cold hands underneath. I moaned with pleasure.

"You still have the same soft skin." Mason huffed.

I wasn't listening. It felt so good. I forgot that we were outside of the pier parking lot.

"Don't stop." I pleaded to Mason. His touch felt so good upon my supple skin. I wanted him inside me, but I didn't know how to ask.

Mason felt around underneath my dress before he found my forbidden spot. I moaned as he applied pressure to all the right places, while being gentle at the same time.

"I've been wanting you since I saw you at the café." Mason said.

"It's yours baby." I said as I grunted in pleasure. Before I knew it, I was tugging at his belt, causing his pants to fall down to the ground. Mason stopped abruptly and lifted his head as if he were listening for something.

"Just making sure nobody is coming." Mason said through heavy breathing.

I put my finger to his lip. No speaking was necessary.

I picked myself up and was now sitting on the trunk of my car. The excitement was heavy. Not only could we be caught, I could also hear the sounds of wild animals echo from the woods around us. Mason spread my legs and slowly pushed himself inside of me. He felt just as good as I remembered.

"Oh, Mason." I said as he positioned himself inside of me. His movements were deep and slow. I couldn't take the heat anymore. I began to moan loudly.

"Mason!" I screamed as he sped up the pace.

"I will never stop loving you." I told him in the midst of pleasure.

Mason didn't say anything, he continued on as if nothing had come out of my mouth.

We both stopped once we heard a loud noise coming from the woods.

"The animals like it too." Mason joked.

I smiled as he continued to make love to me. What we were doing was wrong, but it felt so good. I felt like we were in college all over again. The moon shined bright on us as Mason made love to me atop of my car. I could feel that Mason was about to climax. Just like in college, Mason slammed his body into mine and immediately withdrew himself from inside me as he climaxed. I laughed. Some things never changed. Mason fell on top of me, breathing heavily with lust. I rubbed his head as his body lay on top of mine. It was like we were being transported back to junior year in college all over again. Mason lifted himself off of me and looked into my eyes.

"Do you know what we just did?" Mason asked.

"Yeah, I do." I replied. Do you regret it?"

Mason looked at me and didn't say a word.

"How about we get out of here?" he said.

"Yeah, the animals are scaring me." I laughed.

"Mason, this never happened." I said as I gathered myself to get back inside of my car."

"It never happened." Mason agreed.

We both got into our cars without saying a word. After what we had done, there was no need for any words.

I sat in my car and watched him drive away.

Shit.

There was no way I could face Melissa. How could I do this to her? I was not only a horrible bridal consultant, I was also a bad friend. I just couldn't get over Mason, as much as I tried. This was it. I had to quit. That one encounter was all we needed. I couldn't take anymore, I knew that Mason was not mine. He now belonged to Melissa. Funny I said that after I just slept with him. I drove home thinking of ways I could quit before something got out.

I drove up to my apartment and was depleted with lust and guilt. I don't know what I had for Mason, I wasn't even sure if I was really still in love with him. Honestly, the one thing I wanted was closure. Our session tonight did not help me get over him. In fact, it turned me into an insecure college girl all over again.

****

Melissa walked into Sammie's Restaurant with a light pink maxi dress and her hair pulled to the side. She walked in as if she had a mission. I sat staring at her as she approached the table, thinking that she had something really important to say.

"We need to talk." She said, with an emphasis on the word talk.

I started to shake where I sat. She knew.

"What is it?" I asked her, trying to act nonchalant.

Melissa sighed.

"I need to fire you as my bridal consultant."

I blinked my eyes.

"What?" I replied.

"Yeah, it seems like your work is done here." She said.

I coughed. Did Mason tell her about our encounter?

"Is there a reason?" I stuttered.

"Well, of course, there is a great reason." Melissa said while looking out the restaurant window.

"I want you to be my bridesmaid!" She yelled, causing the entire restaurant to turn our way.

I replied in a hushed tone. Was this some kind of joke?

"Melissa, what the hell are you talking about? I am your wedding planner."

Melissa smiled. "And, a great friend too!"

I squinted my eyes at Melissa. Something had to be behind this.

"What's the catch?" I laughed. Obviously she didn't know about Mason and I. Great. That gave us time to finally stop.

"Well, one of my bridesmaids found out that she's pregnant."

"Good for her!" I shrieked.

Melissa frowned. "Um, no. She found out that she was four months pregnant. How she didn't know that, I have no idea. But anyway, who knows how fat she will be by the time of my wedding! She had to go."

I looked at Melissa in surprise. Sure, she was a little controlling about her wedding at times, but I didn't think she would kick out one of her bridesmaids because she was expecting.

"Are you sure this is something you want to do?"
I asked.

Melissa shook her head. "I know this is
something that I want to do! Be my bridesmaid?"

I sat in silence. There was no way I could be
Melissa's bridesmaid when I had just had sex
with her fiancé under 24 hours ago. I felt so bad,
the guilt came over me. I had to say something.

"Melissa, there is something I need to tell you."

Melissa smiled. "You say yes!?"

I stopped and pondered. It wasn't time.

"I say yes!" I said aloud.

Oh shit.

"Oh my gosh, great! Don't worry, I know we
signed a contract. I will still pay you, I just think
it's only right that my new friend stands by my
side."

"In place of that fat pregnant friend right?" I
laughed. No need to pay me, I'm sure I can find

someone else to fill your spot. Tons of last minute weddings happen nowadays.

"Right!" She said as she gave me a high five. I smiled nervously. Shit was going to really hit the fan very soon.

****

Don knocked on my door the next day, entering my office with a smile on his face.

"Hey, Don." I said to my boss. I was wondering why he had a huge smile spread across his face. He never smiled.

"Ashley, things are about to happen." Don said, still smiling.

I glanced at him confused. If things were going to happen, why was he smiling?

"Oh?" I said curiously. I was anxious to see what Don had to say.

"I found someone." Don said, gleaming.

I was happy for him, but I didn't consider him a friend. I was wondering why he barged into my office revealing his personal life.

"That's great!" I said awkwardly.

"I'm bringing her here." Don said.

I smiled. "Oh, well, I'm excited to meet her."

"No, I meant that she will be working here." Don interjected.

I couldn't believe Donald was bringing one of his whores to work for the company. Mr. Briggs had his women, but at least he kept them at home. I was disappointed in my boss for bringing in a woman that most likely wasn't qualified for the job.

"Have you fired your friend yet?" Don asked, referring to Randy.

"I don't have the heart to do it, Don."

"Well, you better find the heart, or should I say the lack thereof. He's got to go."

"I can't do it. Why can't you do it? You are the Managing Partner."

"Because *you* want to be Managing Partner, and you've got to learn to roll with the punches." Don said with his voice slightly raised. The tension in the room could be cut with a knife. I wasn't firing my best friend that was for sure.

"I don't want the job Don." I said to him. He looked at me as if I had said I was about to burn the company down.

"Well listen, either he loses his job, or you do. I don't know how many times I have to say that. It's time to make a choice. Stephanie starts next week, so he has to be gone by Friday." Don stated matter of factly.

This guy was officially the complete asshole. I don't understand how one of his girlfriends took precedent over someone who worked for the company so long. I didn't want to lose my job, but I had Bella Bridal on my side. I could quit and live comfortably off of what Bella Bridal had to offer me. I was willing to let this job go for my best friend.

I thought of this Stephanie chick and wondered how much of a gold-digger she was. With a huge round belly and a bald spot forming in the middle of his head, Don was the definition of unattractive.

As I walked to Sycamore Park to meet Michael and Thomas to discuss wedding plans, I wondered to myself whether or not I would really give up the job for Ran. I loved Ran, he was my best friend. Would he do the same thing for me? I smiled as I approached Michael and Thomas, who were overdoing their public affection as usual. Thomas spotted me and pulled away from Michael's grasp.

"Long time no see, wedding planner!" Thomas said as they both jogged towards me. These two men looked like they belonged in a magazine.

"We met with your design team, they did an amazing job. We probably should have hired you as our day of coordinator too!" Thomas said.

I personally hated day of coordination, so I was delighted when the pair said they had a family member who would take care of that. I was hoping she didn't back out.

"Just don't forget to send me pictures, I would love to see you two celebrate!" I said.

"Okay Miss." Michael said. "Now, why haven't we seen your beautiful face? We should get full planning so that we can see you more. I'm getting jealous of you spending all your time with other brides!"

"I'm so sorry!" I said to the men. I didn't want to tell them that I was busy with another wedding, that was a planner no go. It was especially a no-go to tell them I was screwing one of my client's men.

He was mine first though.

"Well, here I am!" I sighed. I had no other explanation to give them, so I tried to change the subject.

"My dad won't be giving me away." Thomas said as he changed the subject without me having to. I felt relieved.

"Oh no, why?" I gasped. I figured the reason was because of the partner he chose to marry, but I waited for confirmation from Thomas.

"He told me that he's not giving away a man to a man." Thomas said, holding back tears.

I frowned at how blunt his father was. Even though I have only known Michael and Thomas for a brief time, they were sweet people and seemed very much in love.

"Well, you tell him to kiss your ass." I said angrily, hoping he really wouldn't tell his father those words.

"Ever since I was little, my dad never understood why I liked boys instead of girls. He never loved me for who I was." Thomas said shaking his head.

I embraced my client in order to comfort him. "Michael loves you for who you are, and sometimes that's all you need." I said to Thomas. It was true, in this crazy world, all you need is one person to make you feel like the world doesn't matter. Even though Thomas' father didn't agree, Thomas had what many people in the world yearned for-love. In my mind, he was very lucky.

"Yes, I do love you." Michael said as he smiled at Thomas. It warmed my heart to see people so deep in love.

Now, let's talk about you girl! Thomas said, now in a better mood.

"Me?" I said. I always seemed to make friends with my clients. I wasn't sure if that was a good thing or a bad thing.

"Yeah, you! Tell me about that hunk you were all on at the pier the other day. Is that Brandon?" Michael and Thomas glared at me for answers.

"Yep! That was-"

Oh shit. That wasn't Brandon. It was Mason.

Shit.

I continued. "Yep! That was Brandon!" I said. It was really dark out, and late. I had no idea that other people were at the pier at the same time. Mason and I both scoped the premises to make sure the coast was clear. I was hoping that the two lovebirds didn't get too much detail of what Mason looked like, and I also hoped they didn't see just how far Mason and I had gotten that night.

"You guys really seem to be in love." Thomas said.

I grew shaky, not knowing what to say. I was caught red-handed.

"Yeah, he's a great guy." I kept feeding the lie because there was no way I could get out of it. Brandon and I liked Sycamore Park, we never visited the pier. I never took him there because it reminded me of Mason.

"Well maybe soon, you will be planning your own wedding." Michael joked, playfully hitting me on the back.

More like my own funeral. I thought to myself.

The rest of the evening consisted of wedding plans and once we completed what we needed to, we said our goodbyes and left the park.

After realizing that someone may have caught me with someone other than my boyfriend, I had to get to Brandon fast to save face.

****

To my surprise, I didn't even have to call Brandon when I arrived at my apartment. He was already there. I smiled to myself, thinking that I was going to give him the best sex in the world. There was no way he would think something was up after I was finished with him.

"Come here, sexy!" I yelled out to Brandon as I entered my apartment.

I chuckled as I heard a growl from the bedroom. "I'm here sexy mama!" Brandon yelled. Our sex sessions were never normal. I loved it.

I stopped in my tracks when I noticed there was a huge swing in the middle of the bedroom.

"What the hell?" I said.

"It's called The Love Swing!" Brandon swooned as he motioned me towards him. I walked his way reluctantly. I don't know how the hell he thought setting up a swing in the middle of my room-without permission, would be okay.

Brandon prompted me to sit on the swing. "I like it." I said as I melted on the swings satin cover. It was a new idea-a little weird, but I enjoyed it.

"Now. Take you clothes off." Brandon said.

I smiled seductively as I pulled my slacks down to my ankles, revealing my favorite baby blue lace boy shorts. Brandon smirked.

"The shirt too." Brandon ordered as he lifted my shirt over my shoulders.

I followed my orders and was soon scantily clad in my red lingerie piece. Brandon smiled as he leaned in closer to me for a kiss. Tonight, I was going to give it to him. No more Mason, just me and Brandon. Tonight was going to seal the deal. Brandon kissed my neck and softly sucked it between his lips. The sensation sent a chill down my spine. I moaned out in pleasure.

"Oh, Mason." I called out.

Shit.

Brandon quickly pulled away from me and gave me a look of death. I screwed up now.

"Who the hell is Mason?" Brandon asked, furious.

"He's nobody!" That was all I could muster. I had no reply.

Brandon's voice was raised, and he looked really angry. "If he's nobody, why would you call out his name when we are about to make love?" Brandon was now five feet away from me. I could tell that he was extremely angry. I might as well tell him the truth. Or-at least some of it.

"He's a guy at work that I sort of have a crush on." I confessed, kind of.

"Did you have sex with him?' He asked.

I should my head, "No, of course not!"

I just lied. But what the hell was I supposed to do? I liked Brandon and didn't want to lose him.

Brandon began to gather his things. "Well, since you have someone else on your mind, I think it's time I leave."

"Babe, no, he doesn't compare to you I promise! It's just a harmless crush."

"Harmless enough that you are thinking about him when you are with me? Right." Brandon said as he walked towards the door. My plan for putting it on him had abruptly come to a halt.

"Let me explain!" I said as Brandon left, slamming the door behind him.

I sighed as I realized that the worst was to come. Our cover was blown.

****

The next day I sat in my office not knowing what to do. I couldn't call Mason, Melissa would think something. I was at a loss. I basically had to wait for him to contact me. This was completely getting out of hand, I had my chance to get out and I didn't. Now, I lost a boyfriend, will probably lose a client and ultimately my business. I screwed up. My daydreaming was cut short by Randy running into my room.

"I about had it with that clusterfuck Don!" he said as he slammed the door.

"Quiet down Ran," I told him. "You will alert everyone here."

"Did you see who he brought in here?" Randy asked.

I hadn't. Don told me she would be starting sometime next week. This couldn't be good.

"No, I haven't seen her." I replied. I had a feeling that this day was not going to end well at all.

"Well, apparently she's the intern. He brought her in and said that she is up for the managing partner position. What the hell?"

My lips started to quiver. "Ran, I meant to tell you something. I was looking for the right time, but I think now-"

I was immediately cut off by the entrance of Don and the same intern we were talking about earlier into my office.

"You two, in my office now." Don said before walking out.

"Wait, Ash, what did you want to tell me?" Randy grabbed my hand before we left for Donald's office.

Nothing came out. Instead of me talking, we just walked.

I eyed Don's new squeeze as we entered the office. She was good looking, standing at least 5'7, much taller than Don. She had long hair and big brown eyes. Her tight dress and immodest length heels made we wonder what her motives were for associating with Don.

"Meet Stephanie." Don said, undressing her with her eyes as he introduced her.

"I met her already. Outside, remember?" Randy said.

"Oh, great! Because you will be training her before you leave." Don said looking my way.

"Before I leave?" Randy asked, obviously confused.

The room suddenly squeezed in closer to me. It felt like I was about to collapse.

Don raised an eyebrow. "I suppose that our new managing partner has not told you the news." Don pointed a finger my way.

Oh shit.

"The news? Managing partner?" Randy asked, looking at me with confusion.

"Ashley." Don said.

"What!!?!" I screamed out. I had to stick up for something. I couldn't do this. Or could I? Obviously, I wasn't that great of a person. I was sleeping with my client's fiancé, even after she asked me to be her bridesmaid.

I was a selfish bitch.

"Ashley!" Don's voice was now raised, startling everyone in the room, including his little girlfriend.

"Don I can't do this!" I said. I had to stick up for Randy. He was my best friend.

Don stepped closer to Randy. So close, I'm sure Ran could smell his tart breath.

"Do it Ashley." He whispered.

"No!" I screamed at Don.

Don raised an eyebrow and turned to Randy to do the job himself.

"Randy, we will no longer be needing your services."

Randy squinted his eyes. "What?"

Randy looked at me, disdain took over his eyes.

"This is what you wanted to tell me, why didn't you tell me before!?"

I reached my hands out to Randy. "Ran, I couldn't find the heart to do it!"

Randy moved away from me. "You were thinking about yourself and how it would make *you* look! You weren't thinking about me!

Don broke into the conversation. "Randy you have two weeks to leave the company."

I looked at the asshole I called a boss. "Well you know what, I'm leaving too!" I shouted.

Don smiled. "Are you really? Let's see about that. You need this job."

Stephanie stepped away from us and added a comment. "I didn't know I was going to cause this much trouble."

Don interjected. "Quiet, Stephanie. It was bound to happen. Our managing partner just didn't do it correctly."

"Randy, thanks for working with us, but your time is up. Ashley, congratulations on becoming new managing partner. See you on Monday. Now, get out of my office, both of you."

Randy and I both stood in silence. This was the cutthroat industry we worked in. Great. I could add losing a friend to the list.

"Randy, you are my best friend, I would never do anything to hurt you." I said, looking at Randy.

Randy walked towards the door without acknowledging my comment. "Donald said, get out of his office." He said through clenched teeth.

Great.

I went back to my office with my foot in my mouth, watching Randy leave the office. I wondered about chasing after him, but figured that he had two weeks left. I would quit, wait for him to cool off, then I would try talking to him again. I just didn't know what to do at that moment. As bad as I felt, it felt good to have the words "managing partner" roll off of my tongue. I know, I'm a selfish bitch.

****

A few hours later, I entered the bridal shop to try on my gown as Melissa's new bridesmaid. I had no idea what the hell I was doing, or why I even said yes. Melissa ended up hiring a new wedding planner and everything, releasing me from my duties. I was now a part of her actual wedding party.

The ooh's and ahh's that filled the room told me that I looked great as I stepped out of the dressing room.

"Girl, your ass is so big!" Melissa said as she playfully smacked it. I laughed cautiously. Little did they know the dress was squeezing the living hell out of me.

"Yeah, way too big." Melissa's maid of honor Andrea called out. I swear that girl hated me.

"Thanks girl". I said to Melissa as I ignored Andrea's comment. I wiggled towards the platform to look at myself in the mirror. I gasped when I looked towards my reflection. On the couch was Mason, just sitting on the couch staring my way.

"What do you think Bubba?" Melissa inquired. Mason looked me up in down in a way that I thought was way too telling.

"Yep, looks great." Mason said quickly as he looked back down to his phone. I could sense that he was trying his best to look uninterested. "You will fit in perfectly!" Melissa shouted out in happiness. The wedding was now one week away, and the excitement was just pouring in. "Miss Daphine, come look at my new bridesmaid!"

I sighed in horror as I heard Mason's mother's name being called out. Miss Daphine emerged from her dressing room, graced in a light blue Mother of the Bride type dress. I actually thought it looked horrible on her, and I hoped my facial expression didn't show that. She raised her eyebrows as soon as she caught a glimpse of me, but said nothing. By the look of her face, Mason had not told her that I was the wedding planner.

"Well it's a pleasure to meet you Miss Daphine." I said, giving her the clue that she was not to say anything. Miss Daphine looked at me, turned to Melissa, and then looked at Mason, who shrugged his shoulders. The room became quiet for what felt like an eternity. "Well this is just wonderful! I should have been more involved with the planning." Miss Daphine said. It was obvious that neither Mason nor his mother seemed to care too much about the wedding planning. They would have seen me from the start.

"Oh baby, you look great!" Miss Daphine said as she raised her hands in the air. She still looked the same, even after all this time. And from what

I heard, she still acted the same as well. She was always sweet, but on top of that, she was particularly nosy. I didn't forget about the conversation Melissa and I had about her controlling behavior. I sighed with relief as I wiggled off the platform. This was just getting too real. I knew I would bump into Miss Daphine, but not like this.

Miss Daphine eyed me as I entered my dressing room as if she wanted to say something. I entered the dressing room slowly, hoping not to bump into her after I left the dressing room. I only wanted to be around her among other people. After I finished putting my clothes on, I left the dressing room attempting not to see Miss Daphine. My worst nightmare came true after I saw her exit her room just as I did. "Long time no see, darling." Miss Daphine called out behind me. I stopped in my tracks, turned around and smiled. Before I could open my mouth, Miss Daphine interrupted with her own words.

"Well, this is awkward." Miss Daphine said.

"Indeed it is." I replied. I wasn't as nervous as I thought. When I looked at her all of the memories I had of her came rushing back. One in particular sent waves of pain through my entire body.

"I can't believe he did this Ashley." Miss Daphine said. We were having a phone conversation, shortly after the breakup. Mason ended our two year relationship-and engagement over text. No phone call, no personal conversation. It was simply a text that said "It's over." I was in my last year of college, and I was devastated. Mason had gone overseas and changed completely. I didn't know who he was anymore. "Maybe, he will come to his senses after a while." I stuttered, clearly in denial. I didn't tell her, but I figured it was a long time coming, for Mason had stopped treating me like a fiancé and more like a burden. "Maybe he just wants to spread his wings," I said to Miss Daphine. "I will give him time." I kept telling myself that soon he would come back to me. "Let's hope he comes back before someone else snatches you up!" Miss Daphine joked. I laughed

to lighten the mood, but I knew in my heart, he wasn't coming back. I just couldn't come to terms with it. I hung up the phone with Miss Daphine and cried. It was over, and there was nothing I could do.

I snapped out of my flashback and saw Miss Daphine eyeing me. "Why are you a bridesmaid?" Miss Daphine asked. In all reality, I couldn't answer. "I don't know, Miss Daphine," I said. "Melissa and I are getting closer, she asked me to be a bridesmaid after one of them turned up pregnant." Miss Daphine squinted her eyes questioning my intent before she replied. I could feel that she knew something was up. "Just make sure you are here for the right reasons. You and Mason are long over." She said as she walked past me. A woman that I wanted to call mom so long ago was now a stranger. It felt so weird to be that close to someone one day, and then soon be non-existent in their lives. My heart sank. Why the hell was I here? I shouldn't have agreed to be Melissa's bridesmaid, but it was too late.

Or was it?

I walked outside to the dress shop parlor and looked at everyone together, talking as a family. There was Miss Daphine, embracing her soon to be daughter in law. There was Mason, looking at Melissa as if she was the apple of his eye. That was a look he used to give to me, until he stopped. He would no longer call me beautiful and treat me like a princess. Then, he left me and moved on with his life. So did everyone else, everyone but me. I felt pathetic, trying to hold on to something that obviously wasn't there. These people were not my family, and Mason was not my man. I wanted so badly to run in there and tell Melissa that I had done her wrong, but who was I to ruin someone's life? I loudly cleared my throat and waited for everyone to look my way.

"I'm headed out." I said as I looked towards the floor.

"Oh no, why? I wanted to take you to meet the other bridesmaids and the new wedding planner!" Melissa said.

I looked at Mason, then at Miss Daphine. They were strangers to me.

"Not feeling well at all. I think that bridesmaid dress cut my stomach in half because it was so tight!" I said as I rubbed my stomach. Everyone in the room began to laugh, including Mason. I looked at him and rolled my eyes.

"Well, feel better! You can meet them at the bachelorette party." Melissa said as she held on to Mason.

"Great! Thanks!" I felt relieved as I waved goodbye to everyone in the room. I scurried out of the bridal shop feeling embarrassed. I was a horrible person, and soon I was going to pay.

I smiled when I approached my apartment and saw that Brandon's car was in the driveway. Maybe he wanted to make up. I walked to the door and unlocked it. I found Brandon sitting on the couch in silence.

"Hey babe." I said to him.

"Hey." Brandon said without looking my way.

The room became very quiet. I started to make myself busy and walked towards the kitchen.

"Are you hungry? I've got some leftover chicken from yesterday." I said, pretending as if we weren't fighting.

"No thanks." Brandon said.

"Listen babe. I am sorry. I'm telling you, Mason is nobody serious."

"I don't believe you." Brandon said.

"Believe me babe."

"No."

"What do I have to do?" I yelled out. This whole ordeal was my fault, so why was I yelling? I calmed myself before continuing the conversation.

"Babe, you don't have to forgive me today, but I would like for you to forgive me. Anything I have to do, just tell me." I said.

"I want to meet this guy." Brandon requested.

"Wait, what?" I said.

"You heard me Ashley. Let me meet the man who has my woman calling out his name in bed!"

I walked to the couch and sat next to him. "Babe, I don't think that is necessary. It will just cause things to become worse."

"Did you have sex with him Ashley?" Brandon asked. I wished he hadn't asked me that. The first time I was okay with lying. The second time, I wasn't so sure. I blinked my eyes and lied anyway. I couldn't lose him.

"No."

"Okay. I'm trusting you on this." Brandon said.

"Okay baby." I smiled. Maybe everything was going to be okay.

"Don't let me find out otherwise." Brandon said before he raised himself off of the couch.

"Oh, and I heard what happened with you and my cousin. Are you going back?" he said.

"I don't know." I replied, looking into space. I had so much going on at one time, I couldn't handle it.

"Well, I'm going to bed." He said as he went into my bedroom.

I followed him, but I knew there wasn't going to be any action tonight. I was okay with that. I just wanted things to get back to the way they were.

****

The next morning came quicker than I thought. I knew for sure that I didn't want to go into the office. It was only a few days since Randy was fired and I "quit". Donald was so sure that I was going to come back, but I didn't want him to think that he had that power over me. I also didn't want to lose a friend. I already felt like everything was crashing down on me. Between Mason, Randy and Brandon, I couldn't face another failure. I dialed Randy's number to see how he was doing. I wanted him to know that I would always be by his side. Luckily, he answered on the second ring.

"Randolph!" I shouted, excited to hear that he wanted to talk to me. I quickly quieted down after remembering that Brandon was still sleeping next to me.

"Hey Ash." Randy said. He surprisingly sounded somewhat relieved.

I began speaking before he could. "I'm so sorry about what happened."

"Don't worry about it." He said, obviously being short with me. I could understand why. He was supposed to get fired and I didn't tell him. I thought to myself that I sure know how to screw up other people's lives.

"I was wrong." I told my best friend.

"Yes, you were. I mean, had you been honest with me, I could have found another job in the meantime, or something!" He was right. Briggs Solutions wasn't the only advertising firm in the city, but it was the biggest. Donald thought Randy was a great employee, but he didn't like him as a person. I thought Randy had his days, but he wasn't all bad. He didn't deserve to get treated the way he did. Donald pitted us against each other from the beginning on purpose.

"We aren't friends anymore, are we?" I asked him.

"I don't know Ash. Why did you keep it to yourself? You are supposed to be my best friend." Randy said.

I was obviously a master at keeping secrets. I could hide a huge termination from my best friend, sleep with my client's fiancé and cheat on my boyfriend and had no problems sleeping at night. What kind of person was I?

Well, Mason was mine first.

"How about we do dinner? We can talk about trust issues and whatnot." I wanted to make it up to Randy. Little did he know, I was only trying to protect him. Or save myself from the drama of firing him myself.

Wow. Maybe I really was just looking out for myself, without even knowing it.

I set a date with Randy and hung up. If there was anything I could make better, it could at least be with my best friend. I was going to attempt to make up with his cousin, but I wasn't too sure how that was going to turn out. As I turned and looked at Brandon, he began to wake up. I greeted him with a smile.

"Wake up, sleepyhead." I said, squeezing his nose. I was trying my best to be the regular us again.

Brandon sneezed and smiled. "Morning! Go cook."

I laughed at his demanding request. "I was thinking more of a cereal and milk type of breakfast?"

"That works, as long as I can eat the cereal and milk off of you." Brandon winked as he got out of bed. Okay, we were getting somewhere. I squinted my eyes. "Hey, you asked!" Brandon joked as he headed to the kitchen. I peeked out from the bedroom making sure he didn't come back with cereal and milk and no bowl. He was getting a little freaky again, which mean he was coming back to normal. Hopefully it lasted. I hopped out of bed and realized that it was probably best that I head into the office. I wasn't going to work or anything. Or so I thought. I quickly got dressed and headed towards to kitchen to kiss Brandon goodbye.

"Gotta go babe!" I said as I walked towards the door.

"Okay, see you tonight." Brandon said. Brandon looked at me as if he had a question.

"Babe?" Brandon called my name, looking my way.

"Yes baby?"

"You said you worked with Mason, right?"

"Yes."

"Okay."

I started to shake again. There I was, lying. Technically, I did work with Mason. Just not at the firm. I shook it off, smiled and left my apartment. As long as I didn't hang out with Mason again, he wouldn't find out. I really liked Brandon. I didn't want to screw anything up.

Again.

I walked into the office and noticed that my office wasn't how I left it. I scrambled towards Don's office to ask him about the mishap. Sure, I quit, but he was the one who told me I would be coming back anyway. I don't know why he took things out of my office.

I knocked on the door before entering. "Donald?" I said.

"Yes, Ashley?"

"I noticed that my office has changed. What's going on with that?"

"Stephanie wanted it." Don said.

I smacked my lips. "What the hell do you mean Stephanie wanted it? That's my office."

Donald got up from his seat, looking defensive. I had it coming.

"Correction, that *was* your office. You gave it away when you were trying to save a hoe the other day."

"Don, you were the one who told me I would come back anyway." I said.

161

"Yep, and you can come back. You just have to move into Randy's old office."

I frowned. "Randy's small office? I'm managing partner!"

Donald looked at me with the raised eyebrow he did so well. "Are you? You quit." Every moment with Don confirmed that he as a complete asshole.

"Randolph must have given you the go ahead to keep your job." "He may be your bitch, but I'm not." Donald said to me before sitting in his chair.

"So, Mr. Briggs dies, you become head leader because Mr. Briggs had no children, you fire someone who had opportunities to improve, you blacklist me, and you bring your little slut to work for you. Can you become anymore pathetic?" I asked Don, my voice was slightly raised so that he could see my point.

"Let me tell you something," Don started. "This is my firm now. Mr. Briggs is gone. What I say goes. You can try to fight it if you want, but legally, I don't even have to give you your job back since you quit. Take it or leave it. You see how I got rid of Randy, you could be next. Don't try me."

I became quiet. I didn't want to be next. I thought I had the courage to quit, but I couldn't. The money and power that came along with the job was just too much to give away. And, I did quit. Don had a point. Asshole.

Donald smiled once he realized I had contemplated about what just occurred.

"Welcome back Ashley." Don said as he motioned me to leave his office. I rolled my eyes as I turned and Stephanie at the doorway, waiting to enter. I made sure that I brushed her shoulder as I exited.

I huffed and puffed back to my car after meeting with Don, I figured I could just go back in the next day and move into my new cramped little office. Don's move was great payback, but I was only trying to protect my friend, or myself, or whoever. I didn't know. All I knew was that I was in a huge shit ball. I could feel my phone vibrate through my purse. I picked it up and saw that it was Mason. I wanted to press ignore so badly. I stuffed the phone back into my purse. I wasn't going to answer. He then called again. I couldn't resist. I answered.

"Hello?"

"Ashley."

"Mason."

"Brandon found out about you." I said.

"Who the hell is Brandon?" Mason asked.

Wow, I was so wrapped up in Mason, I never told him that I had a love interest of my own.

"He is my boyfriend." I said. "I've had him for a while now. Before you came back into my life and screwed it up."

"You can't deny that we have unfinished business." Mason said quietly.

"Since when did screwing each other in the woods become unfinished business?" I yelled. "We aren't in college anymore."

Mason agreed. "No, we aren't."

"Mason, we need to let go. I just can't. Not yet." I said.

"Ashley, it has to be now. Soon Melissa will find out and I will lose the love of my life." Mason said quietly.

"The love of your life?" I screamed. My heart was broken. *Melissa* was the love of his life?

"Ashley, she's pregnant." Mason said before pausing to wait for my reaction.

My heart sank. I felt so crazy for still being in love with someone that should have been left in the past years ago. I was a fool.

"Are you sure?" I asked.

"Yes."

There was silence on the other end of the line. All I could hear was my heavy breathing. He just called Melissa the love of his life, and she was pregnant. My heart sank as I remembered hearing some news of my own.

The doctor came into the office and sat down in front of Mason and I with a sad look on his face. We had just lost a baby and we were devastated. "I'm sorry." The doctor said as he sighed heavily. "It seems that this occurrence will not end. You may be able to get pregnant, but carrying the baby to full term is less than 15%." I gasped heavily. Mason and I always talked about having children. Now the doctor was telling me that giving my future husband children may be impossible. "Is there anything we can do?" Mason said as he rubbed my shoulder. "There is really nothing we can do." The doctor said. The room was quiet as I burst out into tears. "What are we going to do?" I said in despair. "We can always adopt. Mason said. I will love you regardless." My heart felt like it was twisted in knots. I knew Mason wanted his own son. The fact that I may not have been able to give him that son broke my heart.

"Ashley." Mason said to me, snapping me out of my daydream. I hated when those happened.

"I always wanted to give you children." I said quietly.

"Let's not go there." Mason said.

"I can't help it! Now you say she is the love of your life!"

"Ashley! We were years ago!" Mason yelled out.

He was right. I had to let go.

I didn't say anything and simply hung up the phone. I cried as the phone slid from my ear down to my lap. I should have been happy, but instead I was a nervous wreck. Melissa was pregnant, and she was going to give Mason the one thing he always wanted. There I was, trying to steal her joy. I was a horrible person.

"Meet me now." I said to Mason.

"Ash, what?" Mason asked.

"Meet me, at Creamy Moos." I said, referring to the milkshake shop up the street. It would be a place for us to meet without sexual intention.

For once.

"Fine. 15 minutes is all you get." Mason said as he shuffled around.

"Gotcha."

Within the next 15 minutes, I was down at the milkshake shop, waiting for Mason to arrive. I shook my head when I saw him, looking great in sweatpants in a tight shirt. He really did want me to jump his bones.

As much as I tried, I couldn't resist him.

"I thought this was over Ashley?" Mason said as he walked closer to me.

"Shutup. It is." I said.

Mason rolled his eyes and ordered a milkshake. "Give me two Nilla-Vanilla milkshakes." I smiled, it was cute how he ordered my milkshake for me. I would have rather had cherry, but I didn't object.

"Like I said, this must end." I told Mason.

"You didn't say that, I did." Mason laughed.

He was right. He did say that. I wasn't sure if I was ready to let go yet. We had unfinished business.

"So, Melissa is pregnant huh?" I said as a teenaged boy dressed in a cow suit approached us with milkshakes in his hand.

"No, I told you that to see if that would make you go away, but obviously that didn't work." Mason counteracted with attitude.

"Why would you lie?" I yelled at Mason. Mason got up and started walking to his car. He motioned me to follow him. Of course, I trailed right behind him.

"Get in the car." Mason said.

I got in the car and put my milkshake in the cupholder. Mason flagged the teenaged boy down and retrieved two straws. He then sat in the car and looked my way. "Why can't we let each other go?" Mason asked.

I didn't know. I wasn't sure why. Did we even like each other?

"Mason, I'm not sure. I just don't see why you would lie-" Mason kissed me before I could finish my sentence. I pushed Mason away before things got too heated. "You lied about Melissa being pregnant. You know what memories that brought up?

"I'm sorry." Mason said. "I didn't mean to. I was hoping that her being 'pregnant' would help you get over me."

Little did he know, it only made things worse.

"Well, I don't appreciate that." I said. Mason grabbed me and kissed my lips once again, causing the two straws in his hand to fall to the car floor. I didn't stop him this time because I liked it. We began to kiss heavily, and I knew where it would soon lead. I pushed his hand away. "Stop being a liar." I said.

"A liar? *You* are telling me not to be a liar? That is what made me fall out of love with you in the first place."

"Excuse me?" I said with anger. I couldn't believe he was trying to turn things on me. He was the one to break up with me. "Let's not get into why we broke up." Mason said. "It's the past. Let it go."

"I'll let go when I'm ready." I said as I reached toward my milkshake. Mason bent in to kiss me once again. I pulled away.

"15 minutes is up." I said as I reached toward the door. I was completely turned off that he would lie to me about Melissa being pregnant. Mason pulled me back softly by my hair and turned my cheek towards his face.

That turned me on.

"Where the hell are you going?" He said as he breathed heavily with lust.

"I'm leaving Mason. I'm tired of this." I said angrily. I had enough. Mason looked at me, unconvinced. He began to rub my neck in soft circles, causing me to moan.

"No Mason." I said as I motioned for him to stop. He could read my mind, because I really didn't want him to stop-and he didn't.

"Tell me you want me Ash." Mason said as he pulled down my blouse, sucking my nipples with a gentle tug. My panties were overflowing with wetness. I damned myself for knowing that

Mason was going to make love to me, once again.

"I want you Mason." I called out.

Mason sucked my breast feverishly, causing my nipples to become harder with each motion. It felt so damn good. Mason then looked at me with devilish eyes and gave me one command.

"Push your seat back." He said.

I obliged and pushed the seat back as far as it could go.

There were no words. Mason got down on the car floor, pushed my cotton skirt up and spread my legs apart on the front seat. He smiled when he noticed that I had no panties on. I gasped as he blew softly inside of me. The warmth of his breath caused me to become even wetter.

"Tell me you like it." He said.

"I love it baby, don't stop." I said.

My legs began to shake as Mason put his tongue in places I didn't even know existed.

"Oh shit baby!" I said as I could feel my walls contracting rapidly. I began to thrust my pelvis on his face, causing him to moan out loud. I didn't care, I was in ecstasy. Two seconds later, it was over, and it was back to reality.

"You taste so good baby." Mason said as he licked his lips.

I simply looked at Mason with hate my eyes and said nothing. I got out the car and slammed the door, cursing myself for letting him take advantage over me, yet again. Okay, maybe he didn't take advantage of me, but I hated myself for becoming intimate with Mason again. He was going to go home and kiss Melissa like nothing happened. I felt so horrible. Then, I felt good in a naughty way. I won. At least that's how I felt at the moment. I remembered that I had to meet Randy at Sammie's, so I got into my car to meet my best friend, thinking nothing of what just happened. I turned and watched Mason drive off. I sucked my teeth and headed towards my destination.

I smiled and waved as I saw Randy approach the restaurant. Randy gave me an awkward smile and looked towards the ground. I frowned. I was hoping that we could fix things and become close again. I wanted to talk to Randy about so much, including Melissa's "pregnancy" and my current relationship with his cousin. I just didn't know where to start. Of course, I chose to leave out the tryst I just had with Mason.

"Hey." He said as he walked closer to the table.

"Hey, Ran." I smiled to warm the mood.

"I'm glad we met for dinner, there are so many things I want to talk to you about." I told Randy. He was one of the few people I could talk to, and I felt like I was losing him by the second.

"Well, I'm here." Randy smiled. Maybe I didn't have to add him to the list of people that hate me.

"Melissa is pregnant. Well, Mason said that he was lying, but there could be some truth to it." I said as I sipped on my martini.

"You mean, the girl whose wedding you were planning, then you slept with her fiancé, then she asked you to be her bridesmaid Melissa? Randy asked.

I gave my best friend a side eye. "Yes, that Melissa."

"Well, good for her." He said.

"Good for her? No! He was mine first Randy!" I screamed. Even though I didn't know if it was true, even the thought of Melissa carrying Mason's child just hurt me to the core.

"He doesn't belong to you anymore! When you get that through your damn head, you will be doing them all a favor! Back off, you are starting to sound crazy!"

I didn't know what to say. Randy was right. I was selfish, and crazy. Randy continued.

"All you do is think about yourself. Ever since I've known you, that's all you think about! You don't think about me, you don't think about Melissa, all you think about is Ashley. Because of that, you are going to be alone for the rest of your life."

"Randy, really?" I said. Our conversation was beginning to be a little louder than I expected.

"I thought we were over what happened at work!" I said.

"We are, I'm just telling you about yourself since you can't seem to see it. You are putting people in danger. That girl loves you." Randy said, referring to Melissa.

I knew she loved me. She would be crushed once she found out about Mason and I. After that conversation, I knew that I would have no contact with Melissa and Mason after the wedding. I would let them be. I just couldn't let her down now. She trusted me, and I ruined it by sleeping with her fiancé.

"You need to tell her." Randy said.

"Ran, it's too late." I replied. Her wedding was quickly approaching, now wasn't the time to ruin her life. Not only had I ruined her life, I ruined my own as well.

Damn, there I go thinking about myself again.

"I can't tell her Ran." I said quietly.

"Either you tell her, or someone else will." Randy said.

He was right. It was time I be honest with her. I had been getting closer to her, and it seemed as if we were becoming very close friends. I was her bridesmaid now, and that meant I would be attending all of her parties, including the bachelorette party this weekend.

"I will tell her." I said to Randy.

"That's right. There's the Ashley I know." Randy smiled.

Good for him, but I was still looking for the Ashley I knew.

Randy and I smiled at each other and ate our dinner quietly. Melissa was bound to find out soon. I was sure that Mason would be the one to drop the bomb.

****

The weekend came around fast, and I found myself preparing for Melissa's bachelorette party. I really wasn't in the mood for strippers and horny women running around. But, I was Melissa's bridesmaid and I had a duty. I smiled as my phone rang, it was Melissa reminding me about the party.

"I'm getting ready Melissa." I said without even saying hello.

"Great! I'm so excited!" Melissa exclaimed. A part of me had a little ounce of jealousy, but overall I felt pretty happy.

"Got your dollars ready?" Melissa said, referring to tipping the strippers at the party.

I laughed. "Yep, all 10 of them." I joked.

Melissa smacked her lips. "Whatever girl! See you soon!"

"Yep, see ya."

I walked into *Sugar Dan's* club with a frown on my face. How could I sit there and watch penis fling all in my face? I was not enthused about tonight's events. I spotted Melissa and a few of her friends in a dark corner. Melissa already seemed wasted.

"You are here!" Melissa slurred as she stumbled over one of her bridesmaids. There was no way that she was pregnant.

"I made it!" I said as I gave the bride to be a hug. I laughed to myself as I saw a huge penis cake adorning the top of the table. It couldn't get any more corny than this. Melissa's bridesmaids seemed to be having fun, they were dancing and slapping each other's asses like drunk college girls. I seemed to forget that we were in a club full of naked men since the girls seemed to be having a party of their own.

"Let's play a game!" One of Melissa's bridesmaids shouted. She was obviously drunk, and it was funny to see the way she behaved. I grabbed a drink and sat down with the girls. I coughed as the drink burned my throat.

"What the hell is this stuff?" I called out.

"What game?" Melissa ignored me as she took a shot. I'm sure it was her fifth one since I stepped foot into the club. One of the male dancers gyrated his way towards Melissa. She slapped his buttock, put a couple of dollars in his g-string and shooed him away. My head began to spin and I could tell that my inhibitions were slowly drifting away.

"Yeah, what game?" I called out after her. I began to feel comfortable with my surroundings.

"Tell no lies." Andrea shouted out. "Someone calls out something they have lied about, and whomever else has done it has to take a drink." Andrea gave me a 'you can't handle this game' look and smiled. That bitch couldn't stand me.

"Bring it, bitches!" Melissa said.

I chuckled as everyone prepared to drink.

"I never told a lie about-sleeping with my boss to get a promotion!" Andrea started. I was disgusted as five of the seven girls sipped their drink.

"Ya'll are little sluts." Melissa said. "My turn, I never lied about sleeping with someone else's man! Andrea, you better drink."

Everyone laughed as they stared at Andrea drinking her shot. Being drunk, I tossed one back too, subliminally telling Melissa that I have slept with Mason.

Andrea noticed that I took a shot and raised an eyebrow.

"Bitch who did you sleep with?" Andrea said.

I didn't know what threw me off the most, the fact Andrea called me a bitch, or the fact that I basically just told on myself.

I swallowed hard. "Oh, you know, nothing serious."

"Well, spill the beans!" Melissa said, curious as to who I slept with.

I was drunk, but I wanted to tell her. Tonight wasn't the night. Not at her bachelorette party. Was there ever a right time to tell her?

"I lied, I just wanted a reason to drink!" I said as I took another shot. That was the only way I could save myself.

Melissa grew quiet for a moment. "Well, all you had to do was drink! There is plenty for everyone!"

The girls laughed, and I felt relieved that my comment was forgotten about. I put my drink down, telling myself that I wouldn't touch alcohol again because it made me too truthful. I looked at Melissa and attempted to bring something else up.

"Well, you are getting married, and I am no longer your wedding planner, I am your bridesmaid!"

The girls looked at me as if they were waiting for me to finish my sentence.

"And?" One of the bridesmaids called out.

"And, I wanted to know one of the things you hate about Mason. We will never tell." I laughed. I looked at the other girls and noticed their straight faces.

"That's not a part of the game." Andrea said as she rolled her eyes.

"Well, hell, I'll answer anyway!" Melissa said, slamming her drink on the table.

"Well, I don't hate anything about Mason, but I do think he may cheat later on in the marriage."

I choked on my spit. What made Melissa think that?

"Why so?" I said.

"I found something in his car that kind of told me that he may have cheated on me."

The girls were all ears.

"What was it?" I said.

"It's a funny thing, it was just two straws." She said.

I looked back and thought to the day Mason and I went to Creamy Moos. We were so busy getting busy that we didn't even drink the milkshakes. Hence, the un-used straws.

Damn she was smart.

"Straws?" I said as I tried to divert the conversation once again.

"Mason knows that I would never go to a place casual enough to have straws in their drinks. I only drink martinis." She joked, but I think she was a little serious.

"That means nothing." I told her.

"It means everything." Melissa said. "He already didn't really pay attention to the wedding plans, but now he may be a cheater. What am I getting myself into? I love him, but I don't want to be cheated on."

I swallowed hard. "It's okay Melissa, he isn't cheating on you."

"All men cheat." Andrea called out.

"Well, we will find that out later. Until then, let's dive into this big penis!" Melissa said, pointing to the awkward penis cake on the table.

"Let's eat some penis!" I said nervously. If she could sniff out two straws, she was bound to find out that I slept with her fiancé.

****

"How was the party?" Brandon said as I stumbled into my apartment. I had gotten so drunk, I had to call a cab home. I felt like I was in college again, but I had to admit, I had a good time.

"Horrible." I lied. The experience was nice, but that fact that I basically told on myself was enough to make me go crazy. I made a mental note not to drink at any of Melissa and Mason's wedding events.

"Doesn't seem like you had a horrible night. You look wasted." Brandon said, looking me up and down.

"I had this stuff." I stuttered, referring to the weird drink I had one too many sips of.

Brandon smiled. "Well, I like 'this stuff'. Want to play club girl gets taken advantage of?" Brandon said as he playfully smacked my ass.

"No!-I mean, no baby. I need to get some-" Before I knew it, I had thrown up all over my apartment floor. I was seriously drunk. My head was spinning and I felt sick to my stomach. Something wasn't right.

Brandon quickly ran to my side with concern. "Babe, you look gray! I think we should take you to the hospital."

"The hospital? Why would you-" I was throwing up again, so hard, it made my sides hurt. I fell to the floor and winced in pain.

"What the hell was in that drink!" I yelled.

"Babe, let's go. I'm taking you to the hospital." Brandon said as he picked me up and carried me to his car-the only choice we had since I had to leave my car at the bar. We arrived at the hospital quicker than I thought, it was all a blur. Turns out, the alcohol I consumed gave me severe alcohol poisoning. I knew I was a lightweight, but this was beyond weird for me. As I laid in the hospital bed, I woke up to find Brandon sitting next to me with a magazine in his hand.

"Hey baby." He said once he noticed my eyes were open.

"Hi." I choked. I felt much better, but I was still a little woozy.

"You've got some visitors, they are outside waiting for you to wake up. I'll tell the nurse to bring them in."

"Okay." I sighed as I closed my eyes, waiting for my guests to arrive.

I opened my eyes to find Mason and Melissa standing above me. I gasped and quickly sat up in my bed. What gave Mason the nerve to show up to the hospital? We both agreed that we would stay away from each other. There he was, with his soon-to-be wife next to him, standing over his mistresses bed.

"Oh, Ashley!" Melissa said as she grabbed my hand. "I was so worried! Your boyfriend called me as soon as you all reached the hospital. Aren't you glad she's okay Bubba?" Melissa said as she stared at Mason. All Mason could do was stare. Brandon interjected and extended his hand out to Melissa and Mason.

"I don't think we have ever met." He said with a smile. "We haven't, but thank you for calling me. I'm Melissa, and this is my fiancé, Mason." Melissa said with a smile on her face.

"How are you?" Mason said as he held his hand out towards Brandon. Brandon frowned and gave Mason a look that could kill. I had never told Brandon Melissa's fiancé's name, mostly because I had lied earlier and told him the guy whose name I called out was simply a guy from work. Brandon looked at me and shook his head. He knew.

"Thank you guys for coming." I said to Melissa and Mason.

"You are welcome, we were worried." Melissa said.

Mason just stood there.

"No need to worry." I said. "I'm fine." I assured Melissa.

"Great! Because my wedding is next week and I need you to be ready." She playfully touched me on the cheek. She was so selfish. It was cute.

"Yes, I will be ready for your wedding." I said to Melissa as I watched Mason stand like a statue.

Melissa and Mason said their goodbyes and left the room.

"You should be ashamed of yourself." Brandon said from the other side of the room.

I looked over at Brandon. "What do you mean?"

"That was the dude whose name you called out that night. Mason, right?"

I couldn't lie. It was about to come out sooner or later.

"Yeah, that's right."

"You said you work with him."

"I do."

"I thought you meant at Briggs and Associates." Brandon said with a frown.

"Yeah I know but-"

Our conversation was halted by Randy running into the hospital room.

"Ash!" Randy said as he ran in.

"I'm okay Ran."

The room was so tense. Second by second, it became harder for me to breathe the air in my constricted hospital room.

"What the hell is going on?" Randy said.

"Ask Ashley." Brandon looked at me with disdain on his face.

Randy turned to me. "Ashley, what did you do?"

"I didn't do anything!" I said. "Look, can we not talk about this right now?"

Brandon cut me off. "Ashley's friend visited her. With her fiancé."

Randy sighed. Brandon didn't have to say much, Randy already knew what he meant.

I made my eyes grow wide so that Randy didn't reveal everything. He knew a little more than Brandon. "Is there something you need to say Randy?" Brandon looked over at Randy confused. Randy was my best friend, but he was also Brandon's cousin. I was hoping that he didn't choose blood. I really liked Brandon, I was just really confused.

Brandon's eyebrows were pressed together, he seemed really angry.

"Well?!" Brandon asked.

"Nothing." Randy said. I was surprised that he had my back after the fiasco at work. I wasn't excited to go back to the office and see what had happened. Things just seemed to get worse and worse. Our tense conversation was interrupted by the doctor entering the room.

"No more bachelorette parties for a while okay?" The doctor said as he came in with a clipboard. Thank goodness, I was being released. I quickly changed from excited to scared. Maybe it would be a good idea to stay in the hospital a few more days to let things cool off.

"She's good to go, she can go home to her loving family now!" The doctor said smiling. He looked confused as he glanced around the room and saw that nobody else was smiling.

"Well then." The doctor said as he awkwardly exited the room.

"I'm going to wait for you to get out of the hospital to tell you about yourself." Randy said to me. I looked over at Brandon. He was shaking his head. I felt horrible to see him so angry.

"Brandon-" I started. Brandon didn't say anything. The three of us sat in silence. Finally, Brandon spoke up.

"You are a whore." He said.

"Brandon!" Randy yelled out. "Now is not the time or place. She could have died yesterday."

"That little slut wasn't going to die." Brandon said. "I gave her the benefit of the doubt the entire time, and this is what she does. She's a whore."

"I'm not!" I yelled out. "Brandon, I care about you, I really do. It's just that-Mason and I have a history that nobody will understand."

"Don't go there, Ash. It was the past. You need to keep it there." Randy called out. I was becoming angry. Who were they to tell me what I could do and when I needed to do it?

"You know what? Screw you both!" I began to yell loud enough for a nurse to peek in out of curiosity.

"Randy, you don't understand what I did for you at work! Don was an asshole, and I was trying to protect you! Brandon, you are completely awkward and I *don't like sex swings!*" Brandon squinted his eyes at me. I immediately began to feel bad. That was a low blow.

"Brandon-I'm sorry." I said to him. He didn't answer.

"I hope you get well soon." Brandon said as he walked out of the room. My heart started to beat fast. Was that a breakup "Get Well Soon?" I looked over at Randy for confirmation on what just happened. "Look at you." Randy said. "You just lost your boyfriend over a man that doesn't even love you. Mason didn't say two words while he was in here. If he loved you like he says he does, don't you think he would have told

Melissa by now?" Randy looked at me, waiting for an answer. I didn't have one.

"I don't know what you are talking about." I said to Randy.

"You do know. It's going to come out, soon. And there will be nothing you can do about it." Randy said. I began blinking my eyes uncontrollably. I couldn't believe what had just happened. However, I was happy that Brandon did not approach Mason in the heat of the moment. I'm sure he knew what that would do to Melissa.

"I kept your secret for I don't know how long." Randy said. "It's over. It's done. I'm tired of it. You can either call Melissa and tell her now, or I'm no longer speaking to you. It's about time you learned your lesson."

"Randy!" I cried. There was no way he could leave me now. He was truly the only person I had. Yes, it was obvious that Mason was probably just playing around with my head. Or was I playing around with my own head? I was completely confused. Brandon had just walked out, and now Randy was about to do the same.

"I'm not telling her." I whispered quietly to Randy. The doctor knocked on the door, interrupting our heavy conversation.

"Your release papers have been signed now Ms. Weeks. You can go home now."

I looked at Randy. He nodded his head as I gathered myself to go back home.

"Like I said, I'm not telling her." I told Randy as I walked towards him. Not only did I want to save myself and Melissa, I also didn't want to ruin Mason's life. I was thinking about everybody in this situation. Or was I?

"Well, maybe I will have to rethink Brandon's description of you." Randy replied.

"Are you calling me a whore?"

"If the shoe fits." Randy said as he walked out. I rolled my eyes, not caring what anybody thought at the moment. I didn't want anything to get in the way of the tryst that Mason and I had. Maybe we didn't have to have sex, but the emotional connection was still there-I think. I didn't want anybody to get in the way. I had to admit, the love Mason gave me was much better than what anyone else had ever given me. If that meant not speaking with Brandon and Randy anymore, I didn't care.

****

The next evening, my heart jumped as I entered the Rehearsal Dinner for Melissa and Mason. The restaurant was very beautiful and seemed fit for a king and queen. Brandon broke up with me and Randy and I were no longer best friends. Meaning, I had to no date to the rehearsal dinner or the wedding.

"You are a little late!" Melissa said as she ran towards me. She seemed to be happy from afar, but once she approached me I could see that she was frowning.

"Miss Daphine is getting on my nerves! That bitch!"

"Melissa, calm down. People can hear you. What's wrong?"

Melissa stopped and looked around me. "Where's Brandon?"

I shook my head. "Don't worry about Brandon. I'm fine. It's the day before your wedding day. What is wrong with you?"

Melissa started to shift around as she rolled her eyes. I could tell she was extremely angry.

"If that cranky bitch of a woman does not leave me alone I am going to scream! She has criticized everything I have done. I thought she would stop. I am going to give her a piece of my mind. Tonight." Melissa said while waving her arms in the air.

I stood there not knowing what to say. I knew how Miss Daphine could be, but I didn't want Melissa to know that I knew.

"Okay Melissa, calm down. Everything will be okay. Where's the new wedding planner?"

"I didn't want her in all the drama, so I'm coming to you." Melissa said.

I reached my hand out to Melissa. She looked at me, ignoring my advances, sighed and stormed off.

Although it was awkward, I knew I had to find Mason to calm his bride-to-be down. After all, I was the bridesmaid. It was time I did something right.

I ran around the restaurant and found Mason standing in the corner.

"Mason?" I said as I approached him.

"Ash." He said with a drunken tone.

I hit Mason on his arm. "What are you doing here in the corner? Go get your girl-I mean, your wife! No wait, actually, go get your mom. She is causing a scene."

"I don't know if I can do this." Mason said.

"What the hell are you talking about? Don't do this again!" I yelled at him. I was hoping that nobody could hear. I figured that I didn't have time for Mason's shenanigans. I turned towards the door to find Melissa.

"Ashley, I'm sorry."

I stopped in my tracks. I couldn't believe what I was hearing. Did Mason finally give me the words I have been waiting to hear? The day *before* he was to marry someone else?

I wanted to clarify. "What?" I said.

Mason stumbled closer towards me. My eyes grew wider as his body inched closer to mine. "I said, I'm sorry Ashley. I'm sorry for just running away. I'm sorry for not being a man and telling you to your face. I'm sorry."

That was all I needed. My heart felt like it released a ton of weight. It was too bad that it took him to say sorry in order to do that. What if I hadn't planned his wedding and bumped into him again? Would I have been burdened for the rest of my life? At that point I realized that he had too much power over me. I didn't care. I grasped Mason in my arms and we embraced in a hug. "Mason, it's okay. I forgive you."

"Kiss me Ashley. One last time."

I pulled away from Mason. "We can't do this! Not again. You are about to marry the love of your life."

"Or maybe I am holding the love of my life in my arms." Mason said as he stared into my eyes. "I was crazy for letting you go Ashley. Sometimes I wish I could turn back that hands of time and start all over again."

My heart started to beat heavily. As much as I tried to fight it, I still had feelings for him. I inched in closer to Mason and kissed him on his lips.

"Hmm." He moaned.

His lips were so smooth, like buttermilk. I knew I was risking a lot, but I couldn't let him go. All I needed was one more time.

There was a moment of silence. Mason began to look around the restaurant hallway and found a closet. "One more time." He said as he put his finger on my lips. "One more time."

"I can't." I whispered.

Mason didn't listen. He pulled my hand towards the closet door. We entered the closet and began kissing each other as if it was the last time we would ever kiss anybody again.

"Oh Mason." I whispered as he put his hands up my dress. I could smell the vodka on his breath. I ignored it, I didn't want anything to ruin the pleasure I was having. I know, I was Melissa's ex-wedding planner. Now, I am her bridesmaid, and she considered me her friend. There I was, having sex with her fiancé the day before her wedding in a dark closet in a restaurant.

Mason's hands cupped my breast, slightly tearing the rehearsal dinner dress that I was wearing. The dress was burgundy, so I quietly cursed him, hoping the tear wouldn't be too noticeable.

"Take off your pants." I said to Mason as his hands enveloped my body. Mason obeyed and his pants were soon on the floor. Mason pulled me closer and slid inside of me. I couldn't help but to gasp out loud. Mason put his finger on my lips to tell me to be quiet. He grabbed me tighter as he thrust inside of me. I have never experienced such passion and pain at the same time. It felt so good. We kissed feverishly and our bodies became one. Mason's movements were so delicate, so gentle but rough at the same time. I closed my eyes and cherished what I believed would be the last moment we would ever share. I felt Mason speed up, knowing he was about to climax. I held him closer to me and put my fingers in his back, slightly scratching him as he released himself. Mason then pulled away and looked me in the eyes.

"I'm sorry." He said.

"Me too." I whispered.

Mason rearranged his tuxedo. We had a rehearsal dinner to attend. Did I feel bad? Yes. Did I regret it? Yes. I regretted everything that has occurred the last few months. At that point, my selfishness took over me. I lost my boyfriend, I lost my best friend, and now I was about to lose something else important to me. I couldn't take anymore. I was so selfish. I walked over to Mason and gave him a deep kiss. Surprisingly, he kissed me back.

"Let's go." I said to him.

Mason nodded and titled his head toward the closet door, prompting me to go out first. I exited the closet, and signaled him to come out as well.

Mason quickly ran out of the closet. I thought that the coast was clear. It wasn't.

Miss Daphine approached the two of us with a sly grin on her face. She held a martini glass in her hand, and by the smell of her breath, I could tell that she had one too many. I shrieked as she approached me during my walk of shame.

"Well, well." She said.

Mason put his hand in front of his mother shooing her away. "Mom, not now."

Miss Daphine laughed. "Not now? Not now? You just screwed a girl who is not Melissa the day before your wedding. Granted, you were supposed to marry the girl first. But, still."

Miss Daphine chuckled.

"Mom, you don't know what happened. Go on to where you were going." Mason stared down at his mother with hate in his eyes. Miss Daphine always knew how to stick her nose in business that wasn't her own.

Miss Daphine looked at Mason, then turned and looked at me silently. I watched her eyes turn in to slits as she said nothing and walked off. Mason and I knew that we had been caught, and there was nothing we could do about it.

"Mason, I-" Mason just stared at me. I'm sure he had no idea what to say.

Mason touched my cheek. "This never happened." He then walked away.

I stood there, in the middle of the hallway, shocked at what had just occurred. I felt hurt and used. Mason made me feel like he still loved me and he simply just walked off. I wasn't sure what I felt. I didn't exactly know what I wanted Mason to do. I wasn't sure if I wanted him to tell Melissa that he still loved me, or if his apology was enough. I watched him walk down the hallway, distancing himself away from me, just like he did those years ago with no real explanation. I couldn't let this happen again. I sat and cried silently as I realized that the man that I had loved had broken my heart once again. Was it my fault? I had no business being with someone else's man. But there I was, trying to claim Mason back for myself. Who was I kidding?

"Mason!" I called out behind him. He stopped in his tracks and walked briskly towards me.

"You heard me, I said let's pretend like this never happened." Mason said abruptly.

"But why did it happen?" I said. I needed an explanation. I needed my dignity.

"I don't know." he said.

I was waiting for him to say something else, but he stood there in front of me silently. I turned my face away from him, disgusted with both Mason and myself. Mason ran off, I'm sure to retrieve Melissa. My heart raged with jealousy, but I knew I had to keep it moving. It was my fault for letting him in. The emotions that built up inside of me boiled instantly, and like a mistress scorned, I shouted out behind Mason.

"I'm going to tell Melissa tonight! Just like you hurt me, you are going to hurt too. You are going to feel the pain that you put me through!"

Mason paused in his tracks and turned back towards me.

"You wouldn't do that." He said.

"I would, and I am." I replied.

I wanted to ruin his life like he ruined mine. It wasn't Melissa's wedding day. Tonight was a good night to tell her. Hell, I figured I would be doing her a favor. It didn't matter to me how my confession would make anybody feel-including Melissa. I was just selfishly ready to relieve some of my own pain.

Mason walked up to me and spoke through clenched teeth.

"You are such a bitter woman and you are going to be alone for the rest of your life. Just watch. I *dare* you to tell Melissa. She wouldn't believe you." He said before walking away.

"Well, you know what? I don't give a damn!" I shouted behind Mason. He was already gone to find Melissa, so I was shouting to empty space. I pushed myself against the wall and thought that naturally, I would start crying.

I didn't cry.

The harder I tried, the harder it was for me to cry a simple tear. All I could feel was rage. I didn't care if I was selfish, I just had one goal on my mind-to ruin Mason's wedding day.

I walked back toward the restaurant and approached the rehearsal dinner. It was my time to confess to Melissa that I had slept with her fiancé. I stormed towards my end of the table on a mission. My heart dropped as I saw Mason hug Melissa and look her in the eyes with such love. That's when it dawned on me. Mason did not love me. He never did. If he did, he wouldn't be here, we would have gotten married years ago and he wouldn't have just had sex with me and turn to kiss his fiancé. He didn't love anybody but himself.

He was just like me.

****

"A toast to the Bride and Groom!" Andrea said as she lifted her glass. Melissa looked at Mason lovingly as they both lifted their glasses. If only

Melissa knew that Mason's hands were just caressing my body about an hour ago. Well, she was about to find out. I think. I quickly lost steam as I realized that I probably didn't have the courage to tell. I sat silently in my seat wondering to myself how I became such a coward. "It is now time for the Mother-of-the-Groom to make a toast!" Andrea said as she pointed towards Miss Daphine. Miss Daphine smiled. I looked over and could see Mason's face shrivel up as if he had just smelled road kill. I was sure that Melissa couldn't tell because she was extremely happy. Me on the other hand, my entire body was shaking completely. Miss Daphine cleared her throat and began to speak.

"I used to always say that nobody was good enough for my son," Miss Daphine started. The entire table laughed at the joke and then suddenly grew quiet. I think everybody knew how overbearing Miss Daphine was, and everyone was waiting to hear what she would say next. The slurring of her words told me that she didn't stop drinking since finding Mason and I earlier that evening. I looked over at Melissa and saw the look on her face, she was obviously still angry about how Miss Daphine had treated her.

"And I still think it's true, nobody is good enough for my son." Miss Daphine said. The table gasped. My eyes grew wide. I couldn't believe she had just said that.

"Mom-" Mason whispered, trying to save face before the shit hit the fan.

Well, the shit had already hit the fan, and I didn't throw it, Miss Daphine did it for me.

"Nobody is good enough for Mason, and nobody ever will be. Hell, sometimes I even think my own son isn't worth shit."

I couldn't believe what I was hearing. Was Miss Daphine about to spill the beans? I glanced Melissa's way and could tell that she was boiling.

"I have had enough!" Melissa stood from her seat next to Mason. I secretly smiled to myself as I watched the drama unfold.

"You are a colossal bitch!" Melissa said to Miss Daphine. I was surprised that nobody had stopped what was going on. I then wondered where the hell Melissa got the word "colossal" from. I was assuming that since only close friends and family were at the table, they let the two get all of the frustration before the wedding day, which was a mistake. Andrea put her hand on Melissa, attempting to calm her down. "Melissa, calm down. Tomorrow is your wedding day."

Melissa snatched her arm away from Andrea. "No, if there is any day this should happen, it is now. Like I said, you are a colossal bitch."

Miss Daphine chuckled.

Oh shit.

I ran over to Miss Daphine hoping that I could get her to shutup. I knew what was going to happen next, a part of me wanted to stop it, but a very small part of me just wanted everyone to know the truth behind Mason.

And me.

"Colossal bitch huh?" Miss Daphine laughed.

Melissa was now standing in front of Miss Daphine, arms crossed. I looked over at Mason, who seemed to be a statue in his seat. I raised an eyebrow, remembering how much of a coward he could be.

"If I'm a colossal bitch, you are a *stupid* bitch."

Mason stood up from his seat. "Alright, you two will not be disrespecting each other like this!" Miss Daphine moved away from Mason, with the smirk still on her face.

"Why is she is a stupid bitch Mason? I think you know why."

"Stop calling her a bitch." Mason said.

Melissa interrupted. "What the hell is going on?"

"Tell her Mason!" Miss Daphine said. I had no choice but to just sit there and let the chips fall where they may. It was time.

"Tell me what?" Melissa said. She was now confused. She figured out that it was no longer just between her and Miss Daphine.

"Tell your *future wife* that you were just screwing her bridesmaid in the hallway closet!"

The entire table gasped and fell silent. Everyone's eyes immediately looked at Andrea, simply because she was the only bridesmaid with a known promiscuous reputation. One of Melissa's family members-I'm assuming Miss Daphine's sister, removed Miss Daphine from the room immediately. Where the hell were all of these people when the fight first started?

Melissa's eyes began to water as she looked at Mason. "Bubba? What is she talking about?"

Mason had no words. There was no way that he could lie, nothing he could do. I sat there embarrassed that my name was soon to be brought up. Even though I wanted to drop the bomb earlier, my anger had subsided. I kissed my friendship goodbye, and then I kissed Bella Bridal goodbye. Nobody would want to hire a wedding planner that sleeps with her client's fiancé. My life was ruined.

Shit, there I was thinking about myself again.

"Bubba, what the hell is she talking about!" Melissa said, her voice now raised. Mason's head was down. "I'm sorry baby." Was all he could muster the strength to say. Melissa began to be irate and then turned towards the side of the table where the bridesmaids, including me, sat.

"Which one?" She said angrily. Andrea got out of her seat.

"Melissa, calm down sweetie. We don't need this. Please stop." She said. Melissa pushed Andrea away. "Was it you?" My head spun as she began to accuse her Maid of Honor for sleeping with her man. Melissa's mom stood beside her, holding her daughters arm as she flailed them around.

"Of course not!" Andrea cried. "I would never do that to you!"

Melissa's mother urged her to calm down.

"Let me go mother." She said.

I had to speak up. "Melissa."

Melissa looked my way.

"It was me."

People at the table stared at the scene as if they were watching a movie.

"Ash?" Melissa said, tears falling down her eyes.

I began to explain myself. "Melissa, if you knew the story-"

Before I could finish, I felt a sting across my face. I cupped my cheek in horror. Melissa had slapped me.

"Get the hell away from me!" She yelled out.

Mason tried to comfort her. She pushed Mason away as well. "Get the fuck away from me!" she said to Mason as she pushed him hard enough for him to lose balance. I looked around at the table. Everyone looked at me with disgust. I felt disgusted, I felt horrible. Actually, I didn't know what I was feeling. I was numb. My legs became heavy as I tried to leave the restaurant. It felt as if my body had become a paperweight. There I was again, with nothing. Andrea approached me with flaming eyes. "I knew there was a reason why I didn't like you." She said as she walked off. I stood there in despair. Who had I become? Better yet? Who have I always been? I ran out of the restaurant and to my surprise, the night sky was beautiful, a completely different scene from what had just occurred inside of the restaurant. As I walked toward the valet, I saw Miss Daphine and the person who escorted her out of the restaurant. I walked closer to them and stared Miss Daphine in the eye. She was crying, and still obviously drunk. I wonder if she was coherent enough to realize that she had just ruined her son's life.

And my own.

No, I ruined my own life.

I couldn't hold my tears in as I retrieved my car from the valet, I didn't even wait to get inside of the car to cry.

"Are you okay ma'am?" The valet asked.

I said nothing as I slammed the door and cried my eyes out, causing the horn to blow after I hit the steering wheel numerous times. I couldn't believe what I had just done, I had just ruined this girl's life. Not only was she my client, she was my friend. All I have done was think about myself throughout the entire process. I didn't think about anybody, not Mason, not Melissa, only myself. I lost my boyfriend, I lost my best friend, and now I was for sure that I was going to lose my business. I had lost everything-simply because of my own actions.

I got what I deserved.

I knew for sure that I was no longer Melissa's friend. I knew for sure that Mason had chosen who he wanted, seeing the way he embraced Melissa as if I had never existed. I picked up my phone and attempted to dial Randy's number. My strength was not there. I dropped the phone when I realized that my selfishness left me with no one. I drove off into the night, embarrassed with what my life had become.

****

It was about two months later, and I was just getting back to normal. Randy still wasn't talking to me, and I understood. I missed Brandon's call one day and even after calling him back at least twelve times, he still hadn't returned my phone call. I picked up my phone and knew that I had to at least make amends with Melissa. Today was the day I was going to apologize to her. Unlike Brandon, she had answered my call and was willing to meet with me. I quickly checked my mail before I left and hopped in the car to meet Melissa. I was nervous as I approached her for lunch that day.

"Ashley." Melissa said as I approached the table.

"Hi, Melissa." I stuttered.

We sat at the table for at least two minutes before another word was said. She looked beautiful. I looked at her finger and realized she had a wedding ring on.

"You guys tied the knot I see." I smiled.

"Yes, we did. I love Bubba." Melissa said.

"And plus, we spent too much money on that wedding. His ass wasn't going anywhere. He told me the entire story. We are getting counseling and we are going to make it work." Melissa said.

I shook my head. "No, it shouldn't matter. I was wrong. Even though he was my ex all of those years ago-"

Melissa interrupted me. "Wait, you were his ex?"

I looked at Melissa, stunned. Mason hadn't even told her the truth. He looked out for himself. She had no idea that I was to be Mrs. Sailors all of those years ago. My heart was crushed. It seemed that Melissa was more into being a wife than actually being loved. Mason surely didn't love her, from what I remember, he didn't even care about the wedding plans. Melissa seemed to have more of my characteristics than I thought. I sighed. "Well, I'm glad things worked out for you." I said as I rose out of my seat. "Take care."

Melissa stopped me before I reached the door. I could see by the extra weight in her face and stomach that she was expecting-looked like about three months. Turns out Mason wasn't lying after all.

"You know, I came here to say that you should feel ashamed of yourself. And if you noticed, I still won." Melissa said with a smirk on her face.

"Of course you did." I replied as I smiled quietly. I was ready to let go.

I got in my car and looked in my rearview mirror to watch Melissa walk to her car. She was going to finish out her life with Mason, a life I wasn't sure would end so well. Or maybe it would. Shit. I didn't care. A part of me was happy that I didn't ruin her life too much. That would give me more reason to better my own. I decided to do what I used to do so many years ago, throwing pennies at the pier. Even though Mason and I used to share that same spot, it was the only way I could close this chapter in my life. I wanted to wait until dusk approached, so I decided to shuffle through my mail in order to kill time. I smiled as I saw an envelope addressed to me from Michael and Thomas. I opened it and a bunch of pictures fell onto my lap. I looked at each picture, smiling as I saw how happy they looked. The setting was great, the people that I hired to set the event did an amazing job. I held back tears as I saw Thomas being embraced by his father, smiling. His father finally came around, and it warmed my heart. 15 minutes passed and the sky began to turn the color of fall leaves. It was time to finally release my past.

****

I approached the pier with my pennies in hand. Dusk had approached and the moon was peaking over the clouds. The water was clear and beautiful. I thought about my life, who I was and who I had become. I smiled, because I knew that there would be a new day. I thought about Mason breaking my heart and how I let one person determine my happiness-for years. It was time I let go. Some people may think that this length of time is impossible, but you would be surprised how your heart can take control-no matter how long you try to break free. I stretched my arm out over the pier and aimed it towards the water.

I threw a penny.

I thought about Melissa, how she was a great person, and how I ruined her relationship, simply because I thought about myself.

I threw a penny.

I thought about Randy, I thought about Brandon and how I lost them because I showed them that I didn't care about them.

I threw a penny.

It was time to not allow the past to affect my future. I had to let go and it took me to ruin other's lives in order to see my faults.

Well, it took me to get caught.

I threw a penny. I smiled as I threw the penny, for the feeling of relief that I used to get so long ago from throwing pennies came rushing back to me.

"What do you wish for?" Mason asked me as I looked over the pier. It was after our first date, and we visited the pier. I liked to throw pennies to relieve stress, and he was the only person that knew my release. "Close your eyes." Mason said as he touched my hand. I obeyed. "Well, what do you wish?" I asked him. "I wish us a fruitful friendship of happiness, and that we never lose sight of what is important. Now, open your eyes." He said. I opened my eyes and looked into

his eyes, wondering what he meant by telling me not to lose sight of what was important, for it was only our first date. When I looked into his eyes, I saw my own reflection. I smiled at him and we both threw a penny into the water.

It now all made sense. The important thing that I was to never lose sight of was me.

The one night stands, the horrible dates, the cancelled wedding, that all made me who I had become, a selfish bitch. I didn't want to be that person anymore. I wanted to start fresh. Meeting with Melissa surely helped. I never met with Mason, and didn't plan to. At that point I knew that the past should be the past.

I choked up and I cried. I didn't pay attention to who was around me. I cried for myself, I cried for Melissa, and I cried for all of the other selfish bitches in the world who suffered heartbreak, clouding their future judgment and hardening their exterior in order to mask their own pain.

I threw my last penny, smiled and walked away from the pier as the moonlight shined down on me. No more flashbacks. I was finally able to leave my past behind. Those people were in my life for a reason, to help me grow. Who knows, maybe I would never be a bride. But I had myself, and I was all I needed. I knew that sooner or later, I would be okay.

You will too.

An Excerpt from D.D. Richard's
upcoming novel

Stray

I don't think I am a bad person by wishing death
upon my own mother. In fact, I think she is better
off dead. Her life has been nothing but a burden
to everyone including herself, and sometimes I
think the ending of her life is the only way she
can achieve peace. I looked around the room and
wondered why God let bad things happen to
people.

"You can see your mother now." The nurse
appeared from the back room with a blank stare
on her face. That's why I hated coming here. No
emotion, no anything, just blank space. I smiled
slightly as I slowly rose from my seat and buzzed
myself in to gain access to a hallway of
numerous rooms with only one small window on
each door. This place disgusted me. The nurse
opened the door to my mother's room and I was
hit with a blast of cold air. I removed my jacket
from my waist and put it over my body, shielding

me from the temperature. Tears welled in my eyes as I saw my mother in the corner, looking at me as if she didn't know who I was.

"It's me, momma". I said as I eased towards her.

She moved away from me, scared of what I may do to her. When she was on her medication, everybody was the enemy.

I was used to this. I embraced my mother before speaking to her. I had to speak slowly, or she would panic.

"Momma, they said you could come home."

My mother said nothing. Just like the nurse, she was empty. A woman who was once full of such laughter, such joy, was now an empty pulp of a human being. Harsh, but that is what I thought.

I sighed. My mother was coming home, and she was now my responsibility. Who knows when she would be back here, maybe next week or two months from now. I was tired of the cycle she put me through, one day she was great, the next day could be entirely different. The nurse came in and motioned me to sign the release papers. I signed them, but I couldn't wait for the next time I was able to put her back into the Psych Ward at Johnson Memorial Hospital.

Made in the USA
Middletown, DE
17 March 2015